"You Going To Give Me That Kiss To Thank Me For Saving Your Neck?" Clint Asked.

Wallis looked at him starkly. He was being logical. They probably ought to kiss. She swallowed noisily in a very casual way, and with her eyes about as open as they could get, she said, "Okay."

She looked at his mouth and his eyes, and his mouth and his eyes again, and she didn't move at all. She watched his mouth smile a little, and then saw that his eyes were brimming with fire. Blue fire? She'd never in her life heard anything about blue fi—

And he kissed her.

Dear Reader,

I know this is a hectic time of year. From the moment you cut into that Thanksgiving turkey, to the second midnight chimes on December 31, life is one nonstop *RUSH*. But don't forget to take some private time…and relax with Silhouette Desire!

We begin with *An Obsolete Man,* a marvelous *Man of the Month* from the ever-entertaining Lass Small. Next we have *The Headstrong Bride*, the latest installment in Joan Johnston's CHILDREN OF HAWK'S WAY series.

And there's *Hometown Wedding,* the first book in a fun-filled new series, JUST MARRIED, by Pamela Macaluso, a talented new-to-Desire writer. And speaking of new authors, don't miss Metsy Hingle's debut title, *Seduced.*

This month is completed with *Dark Intentions,* a sensuous, heartwarming love story by Carole Buck, and *Murdock's Family,* a powerfully dramatic offering by Paula Detmer Riggs.

Happy holidays—don't worry, you'll survive them!

Lucia Macro
Senior Editor

Please address questions and book requests to:
Silhouette Reader Service
U.S.: 3010 Walden Ave., P.O. Box 1325, Buffalo, NY 14269
Canadian: P.O. Box 609, Fort Erie, Ont. L2A 5X3

Lass Small
AN OBSOLETE MAN

SILHOUETTE *Desire*®
Published by Silhouette Books
America's Publisher of Contemporary Romance

SILHOUETTE BOOKS

ISBN 0-373-05895-0

AN OBSOLETE MAN

This edition published by arrangement with Harlequin Enterprises B.V.

® and TM are trademarks of Harlequin Enterprises B.V., used under
license. Trademarks indicated with ® are registered in the United States
Patent and Trademark Office, the Canadian Trade Marks Office and in
other countries.

Printed in U.S.A.

LASS SMALL

finds living on this planet at this time a fascinating experience. People are amazing. She thinks that to be a teller of tales of people, places and things is absolutely marvelous.

To all the editors
that I have had,
and to Risa Goldstein now

One

Tall and rangy, Clinton Terrell was physically hard. His hair was brown and his eyes such a sky blue that a woman could get lost in them.

He was a throwback. He was an obsolete man. If all the machinery at Cactus Ridge shut down, Clint would be just about the only man who could get the place organized and solve any problem.

He was called Lemon's right-hand man on the Covington place out in West TEXAS. But all of Clint's skills, except one, had become motorized or were redundant.

Even so, science was intruding on that one remaining skill. Even bulls were becoming obsolete. Sperm from superior bulls was shipped just about everywhere. The losers were castrated and raised for the market. Who knew what other males would be considered redundant?

In this computerized age, Clint was an anachronism, but he knew cattle. He was born to be a cowboy. He knew exactly how to handle animals. His horses were well trained. He knew how to run cattle and men, and he could keep them controlled without laying too heavy a hand on any of them.

However, his skills had never included proper social conduct. He was rawhide rough everywhere but with the ladies. It was a fascinating metamorphosis to watch Clint meet a woman.

He did know that his herd language wasn't at all appropriate for human females. They'd gasp. And blush. Therefore he was a slow-talking man. Only other men understood what was tying Clint's tongue. His brain was avidly sorting through words, trying to find ones acceptable to women. There weren't enough socially allowable words in his vocabulary.

Clint was not aware he was out of step with the times. He was so secure in his own conduct that he would never have believed he was kept on the place to indulge Lemon's salute to the past. Lemon Covington could afford the indulgence, and he allowed Clint to believe he was the top hand on the Covington place.

While Clint was thirty-eight years old, and a third-grade dropout, it was still possible that he could be brought up to this century. It wasn't too late. The problem was his hostility toward any man who tried to change his thinking or his methods with cattle.

He rejected any male who had the gall to tell him to do things in a different manner. He'd listen, but he discarded changing. He was a stubborn, iron man.

He was opposed to herding with a plane. An airplane was noisy, offensive to the cattle and a waste of gas. It polluted the clean West TEXAS air. But to Clint, any new adjustment of olden ways was suspect. And his language was peculiar. He said things that had only made sense long ago. Like "No bout a-doubt it."

When Clint talked, any Yankee—or those TEXANS who weren't familiar with his speech—had to pay attention. Women did that as they listened to his halting speech and watched his serious grin and his intense, depthless blue eyes. They felt he was shy and they needed to help him feel comfortable. Shy? Clint?

It would take a special woman to bring Clint into even the *taggle* end of the twentieth century. Such a woman would not only need to be patient and kind, but she would have to be very tolerant. With those prerequisites, she would additionally have to have enough sand to stand up to Clint's hard-nosed stance.

When it all began, the year was edging into fall. It was just after Lemon Covington had lured Renata Gunther into staying a while at Cactus Ridge in order to see if the magic between them was real.

On that day, Clint and his hands were out, away from the house and looking over the gathered beeves, counting them and speculating on how many they'd lost.

Lemon said to Clint in an indulgent way, "The problem with you is that you've never looked for a permanent woman. Your life is too easy as it is."

Clint stood by his black horse under the big sky as he looked around. Then he'd taken a deep, satisfied breath and the cleaned-up version of his words said, "It never gets any better than this."

The lover of a sweet, easy woman, Lemon made a dissenting sound.

The miracle of the TEXAS fall was glorious. The days were summer and the nights were cool sleeping weather. The two men stood watching the ranch crew sorting out some beeves. It was a perfect day, peaceful, beautiful, free.

Out of long habit, Clint turned to look farther, and his eyes went past, then back to a dot moving on the far right. It was his dog, Leo. He'd been out and about earlier and then had disappeared. He knew his way around the place.

Leo was a huge dog with a shorthaired yellow coat that was longer around his neck. The dog had once belonged to Clint's cousin.

Clint narrowed his eyes as he watched the dog running toward them. It was serious running. Something was wrong.

The dog got within a reasonable distance and barked once. Then, seeing it had Clint's attention, the dog stopped and turned away, barking twice.

Even at that distance, Clint could see Leo was breathing hard from a long run. The dog barked and backed, turning, and it barked more earnestly as Clint and Lemon approached.

"Where you been, boy?" Clint called as he frowned at the dog.

Leo whined and looked away as he backed up, coaxing Clint to follow. It was very obvious the dog wanted Clint to go with him.

Clint straightened up and looked beyond watching for buzzards. "What've you found, boy?"

And the dog barked twice.

Lemon commented, "He wants to show you something."

"Hell, man, there's nothing to see, on beyond. Whatever it is, it's some long way from here. Look how he pants."

"He's a smart dog."

"S—, Lemon, I know that. I'm just delaying to see how serious this damned dog is." Whistling for his horse, Clint stripped off his gloves as he waited for it to approach. He got a water bag from his saddle horn. He snapped his fingers to the dog. Leo whined and came obediently, but he looked back.

Clint squatted down and spoke chiding, horrific words in a gentle voice. Then he poured water into the curl of his big hand and held it to the dog to drink.

It was a test. How far had the dog come?

Leo drank again and again from Clint's replenished hand. Clint's voice was kind, but his words were blue as he inquired of the dog where the hell he had been? What the — was going on?

And Clint noted the dog's fur was dusty and he still panted harshly from his long run.

Coming alongside them, Lemon said softly, "He's had a hard time."

"Yeah. And he wants me to solve something. Must be a beeve out yonder caught somewheres? Would you take my horse back?"

Lemon said, "Sure."

"I'd appreciate it. I'll take the Jeep." He patted the dog roughly and said, "You get a ride back."

But when the dog realized Clint was heading for the Jeep, it blocked Clint and barked.

Clint looked back at an attentive Lemon. "He's directing my transport?"

"Something's wrong, and the Jeep isn't the answer. I'll drive in and get another horse and follow with some of the hands."

Clint hollered, "Blue? Lend me another rope? Ted, how about your gun belt? And get me that bag of water from the Jeep. I'd be obliged."

Blue was named that because his language was so blue that he was speechless in mixed company. His question was approximately, "What's going on?"

Clint took the proffered rope and looped a tie around it at the back of his saddle. "I'm not entirely sure. This — dog thinks he knows more than me and insists I take Frankenstein instead of the Jeep."

The horse wasn't named for the contrived monster but for the doctor who had been innovative.

Blue's inquiry was something akin to, "Want us along?"

Clint eyed the intensely agitated dog who was staring commands at Clint. "He hasn't selected any of you all. I think this may be a one-man job."

Lemon asked, "That colorfully described dog is smart, but is he that smart?"

"So far as I know, he is." Clint settled the second gun belt around his hips and checked the guns to be sure they were loaded. Then he looked at Blue. "If you don't hear from me in—" he squinted at the sun "—forty minutes, come a-running."

Lemon said, "Here, take the walkie-talkie. I'll follow in the Jeep."

Clint considered the satellite communication unit. It was an irritation. Something like that made him feel attached to a line in the sky and . . . controlled. He said to Lemon. "You can't bring the Jeep this-a way. You'll have to go 'round by the road. That'll put you close to the house. Bring Peanut with you."

Lemon frowned. "I'd have to go clear back to the barn for him."

"By the time you get there, I'll know what we need. Get a winch ready."

"A winch?"

"Something could be stuck. Maybe it's Sam Fuller's low-hung bull got mired."

Lemon looked sour. "It hasn't rained for a while."

Clint shrugged. "It could be a bog."

"Have you ever seen one out this way?"

"Not lately. But I hear tell rain's really coming down pretty good over yonder." Clint pointed with his chin to the northwest. He was readying his horse, checking the saddle to be sure Frankenstein was comfortable. He gave the horse the rest of the canteen water, which he'd poured into his hat. The horse drank.

Standing beside Clint, Lemon looked out over the land. This was high country. In the draws, there were cottonwood and hackberry along with the relentless mesquite. In the low lands, where the winds didn't tear them away, there were the nuisance mesquites monitored by a taller, occasional oak.

The land was rolling and the grasses had scatterings of late wildflowers, but there weren't any public roads and no one lived anywhere close. It was Covington cattle land.

As Clint put his foot in the stirrup, the dog took off.

Clint whistled for his return, but the dog only stopped and stood still. He did turn his head back in order to indicate he was aware of being called.

Clint shouted, "You could tell me what the hell's going on?"

The dog barked once and took off. He was impatient with the man and horse.

Frankenstein went along, pragmatically careful, looking around, listening, very alert. A good, solid, reliable animal. He was unflappable.

The dog was always ahead, but before he went out of sight, he was smart enough to wait so that Clint wouldn't lose sight of him.

Watching the sun, Clint kept track of the direction.

With some irritation, he heard Lemon ask, "You there?"

Clint responded, "Be quiet."

"With your horse thumping along, a voice won't be any surprise. Where are you?"

"I'm going north and about ten degrees west."

Lemon commented, "You'd make a good sailor."

"Land or sea, the sun and stars are the same."

"Keep us informed of your whereabouts?" Not a command. A questioning.

"Yes, sir." Clint was sourly obedient.

"Hell, Clint, we want to help if there's trouble. Is the dog still moving away?"

Clint relaxed a tad. "Yeah. There *is* something wrong, and he's leading me directly there. Suppose it's his bitch whelping?" He was being droll.

Lemon replied, "None has needed help so far."

"I'll call in when I know more."

"Call in your directions so's we can track you. Somebody might be hurt and you couldn't transport. If you go much farther, you might need a plane."

"No place to land. It'd have to be the chopper." Clint kept turning his head. By then, he was some distance from the rest of the hands.

He was alone with a horse and a dog. It felt natural to him. He was supremely confident of his own prowess, and the dog was superior. The horse always considered himself a part of Clint, but more as a comrade than a carrier. It was a calm animal and an obedient one. It would do what he asked of it. Even if both front legs were broken, Frankenstein would try.

Clint patted the horse's neck.

Eventually they came to rougher land. The mesquite trees were thicker. A Jeep would have had a tough time there. The rocks were big, but the track wasn't yet difficult for a horse. Frankenstein picked his way... and Clint heard an odd sound.

It was as if some sundered beast was grunting. It grunted three slow times.

But then it grunted three fast times.

And then it grunted three more slow times. It was an SOS! The international distress signal. What was making it?

He stopped Frankenstein, and they stood silently. The dog had disappeared. The horse blew and waggled his head, rattling his bit's ring connections.

But there was silence. Whoever made the sound had to be human.

Clint dismounted and dropped the lines so that the horse could follow. Clint was cautious. What had made the sound? Why the SOS? What was the threat?

Leo came back to see what had delayed the man. The dog was impatient. So Clint was less cautious. Through the scrubby trees, he came to the rim of a wide, mostly dry riverbed. The roughly centered flow was some distance.

When there was a gully washer, the water would tear through the area and cover the whole basin. Clint again recalled there were heavy rains out north and west of there, and he frowned.

The dog made a sound, urging Clint on, and he led the man.

The horse followed.

Clint looked at the surrounding brush and saw why the dog had rejected the Jeep. And he glanced with some respect at Leo.

Even the riverbed was not smooth. Great boulders were along the way. A tumble of them. The bed wasn't smooth, it was—

And there was the car. It was next to a hummock of earth and stone which had a top covering of weeds, some late flowers and a small, twisted bush. The car was a dusty brown and almost the same color as the rocks. That was dumb. Why was it camouflaged? Well, it probably wasn't. It was probably just such a color because it was an old, rusted white station wagon.

The hoarse sound had been from a dying battery. People were trapped inside the car. They'd been there a while. The car was covered with dust. Why hadn't they gotten out? A wreck? What would a car be doing down in that mess of rocks?

Clint was a recklessly careful man. He would never have driven a car onto a riverbed. Only a really stupid—

And he saw the puma.

So.

It was female. Its dugs were low and full. It was gaunt. Hell. It had cubs in the hummock. Why hadn't she moved them? Probably didn't want to leave the rest there while she moved one?

Who all was in the car?

The dog stood on the rocky edge of the bed and barked. The puma snarled at the dog. Leo looked at Clint.

Clint saw the exhausted puma snarl and lay back her ears. But from the corner of his eyes, Clint saw something move behind the dirty windshield.

He stood slowly, looking around carefully to be sure there was nothing else, like maybe another puma.

From the car came a shock. A *woman's* voice called, "I'm here! I'm so glad to see you! But I don't know what to do. Do you see the puma? She has cubs in there, and the car's stuck. She's exhausted."

Strained of his verbal color, Clint's thoughts were: An environmentalist. Goody. Clint called back, "Who all's in the car?"

"Just me. The car got stuck, and I couldn't pry it out of here. I've used up the battery, sending signals. How did you hear me?"

"The dog heard and came to find me."

"I'll give him a hug when you get me out of here."

She'd hug . . . the dog. Right. With slow word sorting, Clint called back, "What the bloody hell are you doing out here all by yourself? Do you have any idea how many yahoos there are out here, running around loose? Anything could happen to a stupid female that got herself stuck in a wash thisaway. Are you stupid, along with being dumb?"

She rolled down the window a bit more and silently brought out the ugliest looking, snub-nosed gun and pointed it right at his stomach as she said, "Bang!"

His guns were old Colts with cylinder load. Hers was black, square and nasty looking. Who was she? Where would a nice woman get a gun like that? "What're you doing out here?"

"I'm a horticulturist."

He knew the word meant plants. She probably meant marijuana and she was a runner. She'd used the other word to try to fool this nice TEXAS boy? He waited, but apparently she believed she'd replied sufficiently.

"Why are you out here, alone thisaway?" His voice had a hard edge. He was going to have to do something about rescuing a stupid woman who was where she shouldn't be.

She understood he was annoyed. With exquisite patience, she replied, "To collect flora peculiar to the area?"

She collected flowers? "Didn't your mama ever tell you not to go gallivanting off by yourself?"

"She's in Somalia?" That was the questioning, do-you-understand statement. "I couldn't reach her for permission." The not-yet-rescued woman spoke in a very kind way.

He snarled at her. "If you plan for me to get you out of this here mess, you'd better change your tone."

"Yes, sir."

Twice, now, Lemon had tried to contact Clint. Clint finally lifted the mouthpiece and said, "Not yet. Stand by."

Then he said to the female, who was in a nasty trap, "Can you walk? Are you in any way hurt? Can you move?"

"I just need you to carefully distract the distressed mother and make her understand that I'm not after her babies."

The environmentalist had spoken.

She continued, "Then I'll leave the car and you can direct me to the nearest McDonald's."

"You got water?"

"Yes. But I did neglect to bring along enough food."

"How long you been out here?"

"This is the third day. The little mother must be starving. She's been so vigilant. Have you any food to leave for her?"

Clint looked at the river and said, "She's had water."

The woman's voice responded, "None from me. The river's nearby. I assume she has. I tried to get out of the car a couple of times and leave her here, but she didn't understand that I don't want her babies." Then she added, "We're upsetting her terribly."

He'd noticed. Leo was watching alertly. So was Frankenstein. He called, "How much do you weigh?"

"Do gentlemen ask that?"

"I'm gonna have to lift you up on the horse."

"I actually weigh one hundred, fourteen and a half pounds."

Little. Clint called back, "I can handle that." Then he asked, "Is there anything in the car that you absolutely got to have? And can you leave the door open so as the puma can see it's no threat?"

"Nothing is vital . . . but me."

He muttered, "Of course."

"What?"

"I was agreeing. I'm gonna get the dog to distract the puma, and I'll come in with the horse. Do you understand." That was a statement. "Get on the other side of the car. Be ready to come out the door. The path is reasonable. We'll go on down to the water and over thataway, down stream and back up onto this rise and away. Get ready."

Then Clint said into the remote, "Did you hear me?"

From the satellite piece, Lemon said, "Are you sure?"

"Yeah."

Lemon asked, "How're you gonna convince Leo to do as you suggest?"

"He and I have hand signals? He'll understand."

Lemon urged, "Try not to hurt the puma. The papers I'd have to fill out are staggering."

"Yeah."

"Good luck. Keep the circuit open so as we can hear."

Clint declined. "I can't be distracted. I'll let you know how it comes out. You're a bunch of shh-snoopy buzzards."

"Yeah. Good luck."

Clint hollered to the woman, "Get ready."

"Ready!"

Then Clint squatted down by the dog and held Leo's head to look. He gestured. Then he said, "Sic'em." And he looked at the dog seriously. He repeated the gestures and the word. Then he stood up. "Stay."

Leo watched him, shivering with held tension.

Clint went over to Frankenstein and climbed on board. Then he gathered the reins and began the careful descent down the rocky slope. He got almost all the way down. The puma was very upset, ears back, snarling, in a crouched prowl, about to attack, when Clint gestured.

Leo came down the slope snarling and barking and was . . . impressive!

Clint lost no time, at all, as he urged Frankenstein toward the car. The horse was aware of the threat of the puma, but he did as Clint's knees directed.

As they reached the side of the dirty car, a form erupted from it. Frankenstein hesitated long enough for Clint to lean over, grab her lithe figure and hoist her up behind him onto the horse's backside.

Clint told her, "Hang on! This'll be rough."

He was instantly aware of her body against the back of his. And her slender hands were clasped tightly around his middle.

From the other side of the car, there were snarls and deep barks and one yip! Frankenstein went on past and off toward the slight actual river. They got there with Clint yelling for Leo, who came running barely ahead of the puma!

With the woman clinging to him, Clint whirled the horse and charged the puma. Clint lifted his gun free and fired it into the air and hollered the rebel yell.

The puma was outnumbered and crouched as the horse went aside and off with the dog, then, leading them.

It was over.

Once around a screening bend, they went more slowly. Frankenstein had to pick his way among the rocks by the stream. Clint asked over his shoulder, "You okay?"

She was shivering from reaction. "Your rescue was brilliant! You've trained your animals exceptionally."

She was giving most of the credit to the horse and the dog. He considered. She was right. He said, "I trained them to mind me."

"They do it well."

They went on in silence. He found his attention was concentrated on her. He wanted to turn around and look at her, but to do it would seem . . . interested, so he did not. She smelled of "woman" and his body was riveted. She was probably so ugly she wouldn't need a mask on Halloween. He'd have to check her out before anyone else saw her. How? His clever tongue asked, "Want to swim?"

"Do I smell . . . a little . . . ripe?"

"Not nearly like any man I've ever been with. I thought you might want to be in the water." She'd been in that car for three days. Then, in a voice that was a little husky, he added, "You sure do smell like a woman."

"That's sweat."

She was an innocent. After a small silence, he said, "I don't smell any—" he sought an acceptable word "—urine, how'd you . . . manage . . . being a woman."

She was startled he'd mentioned something so personal.

"I have—had—an empty tomato can."

"Oh." His mind saw her using it. She would empty it out the car window, and the puma would smell the new scent and be freshly alarmed.

They went farther down the river, farther from the puma. There were only rocks and gravel, which water had spent long ages smoothing. It was an old riverbed. The water was clear.

He asked again, "Do you want to rinse off?" She could take off her clothes and swim. He wouldn't mind.

"It would be wonderful. I'm trying to believe I'm out of the car and this isn't a dream. I dreamed last night a man on a black horse rescued me. Is this the dream, still?"

"No."

"I'm really out of the car?"

"Yes."

"I believe I'm going to cry."

He replied logically, "You're probably too dehydrated to make tears."

And she laughed in hiccups.

Frankenstein stopped, and Clint swung his leg over forward and slipped down. He petted the dog and examined him. Then he bragged on the dog as he reached up and lifted the woman down.

She was young. She had a strange-looking gun belt over her shoulder. She was lithe and shorter and easy to handle. She was sunburned and a little strung out. Three days alone. She had gotten to the point where she was going to either run out of water or risk leaving the car.

She turned toward his dog, but she spoke to Clint. "May I touch him?"

"Sure."

"What's his name?"

"Leo."

She knelt down and extended the back of her hand toward the dog to smell her. "Hello, Leo."

Leo accepted the chance and moved his nose forward to sniff her hand.

She told the dog, "I owe you a big one. You went all the way, somewhere, to find help for me. Thank you."

"He's my dog."

She looked up at the man. "Thank you for coming with him to get me out of there."

"You're welcome." Clint watched her very seriously. "What's your name?"

"Wallis Witherspoon."

He almost smiled as the wrinkles around his eyes deepened. "Mine's Clint Terrell."

And she responded formally, "How do you do?"

"Better'n you. Want to splash some water over your face?"

"I want to lie down in it."

"Go ahead. It might be a little cool." Then he warned, "You could get cold."

"It would be wonderful!" She rose from her knees by the dog and looked out over the shallow river.

She was going to strip and swim? Right here? His breathing picked up.

Away from the slow main current, the water along the shallow edge was sun warmed. She put the gun belt on a flat rock.

Still in her cotton trousers and shirt and wearing her tennis shoes, she waded into the river's edge.

He stopped her. "You can't go out thataway, there could be quicksand." He found a stick so that she could test the bottom.

But she hadn't intended to swim.

There were all sizes of rocks in lumps above the surface of the river. It looked safe and easy. She walked into the shallows. Still in her clothes, she sat in the water, then lay back. Her face was above the water, so were the islands of her flattened breasts, so were her hands, which were resting on her stomach and, on down, her knees and the toes of her tennis shoes stuck up individually.

How irritatingly modest of her to keep on her clothes. Well, he'd done that—summers.

Wearing his boots, Clint sloshed carefully into the river and stood over her. He was watching for water moccasins—the snakes were deadly.

He noted her features were regular, she was attractive, her body was female. He glanced around the area carefully. He looked back at her. Her little gasps were erotic. Her shirt was wet and revealed her upper body. She was nicely female.

Her hair was black, and the water curled it lazily as it floated around her head. She wore no makeup. Her eyelashes were naturally dark. She lay in the water with her eyes closed.

He said nothing. He was silent and waited. Actually he could have said anything at all, and she wouldn't have heard him. Her ears were underwater. While the water didn't submerge her entirely, she couldn't hear.

At the edge of the stream, the dog lapped the water and sat, panting, and Clint knew the dog was exhausted. Leo was the main reason for the delay in getting her to the house. The dog needed to rest. The other reason was Clint's surprise interest in the woman. He wanted her to himself for a while.

Frankenstein moved slowly, nuzzling the grasses, getting a mouthful here and there, and he came to the edge of the water to drink.

It was silent and peaceful.

The remote asked, "You all okay?"

Clint replied, "All okay."

"Who all was in the car?"

"One. And the puma is okay. It would be kind of you to drop some raw meat close by. We're just above Stephens's Crossing. There's a rock hummock by the left bank past the curve. Put the meat up on the bank, but not too close. Drop it from some distance up. The cat's really spooked and really tired."

Carefully, Lemon inquired with some irony. "The one rescued . . . is it okay?"

"Soaking in the river, dehydrated and very tired."

Lemon asked, "You coming to the house?"

"When she can."

Lemon's voice was slow and very soft. "She?"

"Yeah."

Two

The remote satellite communication in Clint's pocket said, "Over west of here, the word is there's a gully washer runoff that's coming along your way. You'd best get to high ground."

Clint told the intrusive gadget, "I hear you."

"She . . . okay?"

It was only then that Clint connected the rescue of this woman with Tweed Brown's rescue of his Connie just the year before. So Clint's voice was fairly kind as he replied, "All's well."

Lemon cautioned, "Don't lag. The report says it's really coming."

Clint glanced down. With her eyes closed, and her ears underwater, she had no idea he was communicating with anyone.

Clint looked over to the northwest and said into the remote, "It's coming, all right, and in a hurry. We might have to make the line shack do for a while. She was trapped three days and isn't too perky."

"The line shack? That's on the other side of the river. You could go—"

"I hope somebody was smart enough to check on supplies?"

"I'll find out." Lemon sounded serious.

Clint scoffed. "We'll know before you do. I'll be in touch."

"Take care of her."

Clint saw no reason to have to reply. He leaned over and touched her clasped hands lying on her stomach.

She opened her eyes. They were purple. The irises were really unusual. He was fascinated. They stared at one another.

He pointed to the northwest.

She had to lift her head to look. While the heavy clouds were thick along the horizon, she couldn't see them from that vantage point. She looked at him in question, and Clint saw the limestone stain in the middle of the still-shallow river. The stain was the first indication of the flooding to come.

He motioned for her to stand up, and she did that. Then he said, "There's a storm's flood a-coming."

Being shorter, she could barely see the top of the black clouds. But the line of them was long, so the storm was vast. Even she knew that.

He told her, "There could be a flood. We got to get across before the first wave hits. Hurry!"

"Why are we crossing? You didn't come from that direction."

"There's a line shack over yonder that'll have food. The storm'll be here pronto."

He whistled a shrill command, and the horse came without asking if it was necessary. That was something. Leo, too, was watching the horizon, sniffing the air.

Clint took his jacket from the strings at the back of his saddle and put it on her. He gave her his bandanna from around his neck and said, "Put this on your head." In his collection of experiences with women, they chilled easily. He added, "You're wet, so you'll be cold."

She shook water from her hands and squeezed out her shirttail.

That was erotic. *That* was? He was in sad shape.

She looked up at the clear sky; then her gaze went to the horizon.

He saw her pupils widen.

She looked at the river and she, too, saw the widening stain.

Clint lifted her up onto the horse's rump, and she settled there. Clint slung her gun belt over the saddle horn. He immediately slid into the saddle, swinging his leg forward with practiced ease.

She wondered how many times he'd had to carry something on the back of his horse that he could be so agile and smooth in doing something that awkward.

He whistled for the dog, who had logically thought they were going the other way. But he did follow.

They started across the river. Leo had to swim in the middle of it. Beyond, in the far distance, they could hear the muted roar of the approaching gully washer.

The sound was attention getting. Wallis had heard of such, but now she would see it. She was stimulated and turned her head, keeping track of the river and the dog. She said, "Hurry."

In his frustrated slowness, he warned, "Potholes. We've got to be careful or Frankenstein could dump us, and we'd be drowned."

"In that case, be careful."

In a stern filtering of words, he told her, "I know what I'm doing."

And she had the gall to say, "Of course."

Then Clint said softly, "Look." And he pointed upstream. From where they were, in the middle of the riverbed, they were beyond the curve that had hidden her car. They could see it. The car was quite small at that distance. She was puzzled and looked again at the car, but something moved beyond it.

Wallis could barely make out the puma herding her three kits up the side of the bank and out of danger. The cat was still nervous of the car and kept crouched and ready as she looked back at it.

The tiny kittens wobbled along with their ears back, obeying, getting away from all the dangers. And the little family was quickly out of sight.

Softly, Wallis said, "Poor darling."

And Clint turned his hard face slowly, so that he looked at her over his shoulder. His blue eyes rested on her. He saw her shiver, and her hands on his stomach were cold. She was cold? Just from a little dip in the river? She already had his jacket and she was still shivering!

Then he thought of all the times he'd been out and about and gotten soaked . . . and hadn't paid any attention to it. Women were fragile.

As Frankenstein moved from the riverbed, Clint took off his Stetson and put it on the kerchief that covered her wet head. He told her, "Run the catch up under your chin so's you don't lose my hat."

Awkwardly she obeyed his directions. She got it too tight and couldn't get it loosened. He turned sideways in the saddle and showed her fingers how to release the stay so that she could clamp the strings wherever she wanted.

He smelled good.

It was an interesting thing for her to notice. He smelled not of horse but of the out-of-doors. He smelled male. But he smelled of fresh male. She resisted putting her nose against his back and inhaling deeply. He'd think she was some kind of nut.

So she was discreet. He smelled good to her. She smiled just a trifle with no outward sign of it, and she was proud of herself for being discreet.

He knew she was investigating his back. She didn't choke or cough. She didn't move farther back onto Frankenstein's haunches. That she stayed put was stimulating.

With the distant, roiling clouds and the freight-train water roar escalating, Frankenstein was somewhat edgy. Clint talked to him in the nicest soothing way. He used sounds instead of blue words like he generally did. He gently guided the horse to the highest point he could see. It was close enough.

Without the woman, he would have galloped away from the river. No, he would have gone back to the house. The woman was the reason he was on the wrong side of the river. Wallis, her name was Wallis. And he wondered if it was spelled the way a man spelled his name?

For Wallis, to be out of the car again was wonderful. To witness the strong, positive movements of the dog, the horse and the man in such a setting was thrilling.

She looked around with great visual appreciation. The area was beautiful. It was eye filling to see the amazingly subtle colors in the water, of the grasses, the flowers, the rocks and the lacy trees against the brilliantly peaceful sky overhead. With the low, restless clouds peeking over the horizon, it was a natural panorama that was wondrous. Brain swamping.

The building of the roar was nerve shivering. She asked, "Are we high enough?"

He replied, "We'll see."

But there was no readily accessible place that was higher.

He felt her shift as she discreetly checked out his evaluation of the terrain. Sassy. They were called "new women." She considered herself equal to a man? His mind smiled. She was the one shivering and holding on to him.

The leading edge of the gully washer came into view. It was spectacular! It looked...natural...a part of the wild, untenanted land. It was as if the witnesses saw something powerful happening that wasn't devastating.

Without people and their animals and crops, their houses, roads and cars, nature's variances were a natural thing. Its fires cleaned the land, eruptions replenished the soil, wind and floods distributed seeds with the water.

The "disasters" had a purpose. This is a live planet. Its live volcanos or hurricanes or earthquakes all were for a reason. They only inconvenienced humans. Animals just moved aside or ran away.

But the gully washer's power was awesome.

Clint was as intense as she. With calming sounds and gentle hands, he soothed Frankenstein perfectly. The horse was alert, curious and watching just exactly as they were. And so was Leo.

The double-ridden horse with the dog to one side was like a model for a Remington bronze.

Since the riverbed was so wide and the last gully washer had cleared brush away not too many years back, the watchers could see far enough upriver as the brunt of the flood came toward them. It was incredible.

There was nothing around there that could be harmed by the coming onslaught of water. Under the still calm, mostly blue sky, the flood crashed along in great expanding waves that hit over the sides of the banks and splashed away, but the main snake head of the flood never appeared to diminish. It came on.

Clint told her passenger, "We're out of reach."

She shivered. She was excited and her arms tightened on Clint's body. He was already aware of her as a female. Her excitement over the panoramic view of the powerful gully washer was stimulating enough without her hugging her body against his.

The head of the flood went past at a train's speed, and it sounded like one. It was really something to see. And while the side waves came almost to their rise, the surge went around them and on past into the dips and runnels of the land.

The main stream was swollen with dirty, turbulent floodwater. Trees were trapped in the headlong surge, rolling helplessly, catching and being torn away to ride free.

The basin was brimful and very swift. It would be stupid to try to swim a horse across it. It would be worse at that point for a person to try to swim it. It wasn't just swift, it was cluttered with debris, which made it dangerous.

Clint told his passenger, "We need to stay put a couple of minutes. There might be a second surge."

With pale lips, she said, "Yes."

The river would take days to settle down. Clint could have taken her back to Lemon's place. It would have been a long ride, but she and Clint could have gone there. He had chosen to keep Wallis isolated until the river went down, enough.

His dark hair and his shirt collar were ruffled by the breeze from the passing rush of water. The bottom of his face was brown from the sun. His forehead was white from the shading of his Stetson.

He moved his head slowly and looked around his shoulder at her face under his hat.

Under his Stetson, her eyes were out of sight, but her bluish lips said, "Wow. I am impressed. I've read of gully washers, but this was really something! Thank you for getting me out of the car. I'd have drowned."

His deep, soft voice replied, "It was Leo did it. He just got me to help him."

"If you hadn't gotten me away, the puma mother would have stayed with her cubs and she'd have drowned—too."

"Maybe not. She knew it was coming."

"How could she have known?"

He replied with slow logic, "She got them out. She couldn't see upstream. She could feel it in her feet. And she could very probably hear it coming. When you were soaking, I could feel it. The sound was just beginning."

"You didn't mention it. You let me soak."

"You needed to be calm."

"I'm freezing."

He was silent for a minute as he watched her. Then he said in a soft, husky voice, "I'll get you warm."

She blinked at his words, but remembered he'd said there was a line shack. He'd meant they'd go there and he'd build a fire.

Clint spoke into the remote. "The gully washer's passed above Stephens's Crossing."

See? He was reporting in to his people. He had nothing else in mind but getting to the line shack.

It was Teddy monitoring the remote. "You guys okay?"

Clint replied, "High and dry 'til the rains hit."

She looked over at the horizon. The clouds were higher. They were restless in such a way that she knew the winds would be harsh when it hit them. She shivered. She was already wet and cold.

But she noted the horse watching around like an interested wild horse. Most horses she'd known hadn't been very alert. They'd minded and been bored and plodding. Frankenstein was not bored.

She considered how revealing it was about a man whose horse wasn't a plug. The horse was a partner. So was the dog. It, too, was an alert animal. Look what the dog had done about her. When he hadn't been able to distract the puma by himself, he'd gone for help.

It had been a remarkable day.

She was so chilled that her teeth had to be clenched to keep them from rattling. But she shivered.

He said it again, "I'll get you warm."

To a woman in those circumstances, how much of a recommendation was a dog's trust of a man?

Who was this man? Was she out of a trap of one kind to be caught in another? Her mother's stern advice was to never get herself into a position to be raped. The wordage was succinct.

So. She was going to sleep in a chair while he had the bed? Yep. How droll. Well, she still had kinks from being trapped in the car, so it would probably be just as well that she'd have to squirm around in a chair. She needed the exercise.

Only then did she realize she was plastered against Clint's warm back. How stupid. She straightened, but the horse suddenly started bouncing in a strange lope. She had to clasp Clint again to keep her balance—but then the horse settled into an easy stride again.

Hmm.

Was this Clint person being clever? Was he being underhanded and sly? Was he taking her to some salacious hideaway, this so-called line shack, with ulterior motives? How come they weren't on their way to his headquarters?

"Why are we going to a line cabin?"

"It's too far to the house by horse."

"How far?"

"Double this way, it would be dark. It's going to storm and—"

"But the storm isn't—" She had leaned back to look to the northwest, and the clouds were higher in the sky! In the stillness, it was strange to see the clouds tumbling so restlessly. The turbulence was a contrast to the stillness where they were.

Although it was at a distance, there was an attention-getting crack of thunder, right on cue!

She was silent. She curled up against him again and shivered.

"You cold?"

"I think it's nerves."

There was a pause while he sorted out why she should be nervous. He told her, "You probably shouldn't have soaked in the river. You're cold."

"I was dehydrated, and I had to soak up some moisture so that I wouldn't crack if I smiled or turned my head or tried to walk."

She saw his cheek puff so she knew that he smiled. He denied she was dehydrated. "You said you'd had a month's supply of water."

"I did. But being inside the car was like living in a solar-heated tin can with the windows mostly up and the puma prowling around."

"You had a gun."

"How could I shoot a mother?"

"Would you have? If the month was up, and there was the choice between you or the puma, would you have shot her?"

"The way I had it figured, by then she would have become accustomed to me and trusted me, or the babies would have followed her off, completely okay, in the middle of some night."

"You'd've done that for a puma?"

"Her kind's endangered—mine's not."

They could hear the front coming from far away. In such a place, there was nothing high enough to stop the winds.

He said, "Hold on to my hat. And close your eyes. Put your face against my back. The dust'll be thick."

It was strange, for the wind came just like the pent-up, hurrying wave of water in the gully washer. There were no heralding winds. It was a front and it came as one. It was a wall of wind, which hit them with dust and twigs and torn-off leaves that pelted them.

Clint turned the horse away, not only to protect the horse's nostrils and eyes...but his own. She had his jean jacket and battered Stetson hat. She clutched the hat tightly with both hands as she crowded against his back.

Clint liked that.

He was startled to feel pleasure just because she was pushing against him, seeking shelter from him. In all his years, he'd never wanted anything like that from any woman. He liked a woman to be attentive and willing. Until now, that had about covered it.

With her burrowing against him in the force of the wind's buffeting, his body wanted to turn and take her against him...to *protect* her! To shelter her. It was very odd for him to feel the need to shield a woman in such a way.

He moved the horse toward the line shack. The horse really wanted to just drift with the wind at his back. Such drifting was natural to a grazing animal. That's why cattle piled up and died at barriers in the blue northers.

The dog would have gone along with the wind at his back. As it was, Leo trotted beside Frankenstein, using the horse as a partial screen from the force of the wind and the debris it carried.

She said, "You should wear your hat. I can put your jacket over my head."

So he took the wind-agitated hat carefully from her hands. He put it on firmly and pushed the two-strand holder up the strings and under his chin.

Then he felt the warm barrier of her against his back, huddling close to him. He looked around as if he owned the universe. And he smiled at himself.

In his time, on occasion, he'd carried women on the back of his horse. It had been an ordinary thing to do.

He'd been aware of the women and felt their soft bodies against his back. He'd talked to them and listened, but it hadn't been with the feeling he had at this time, with this woman.

The impulse to bring her across the river and trap them on this side had probably been a stupid thing to do. He was only a cowboy. He had little schooling.

She was a different woman. At the big house on Lemon's place, Clint had been around a lot of different women who were Lemon's guests. He got along with them all right, flirting, teasing, dancing, loving, but there'd never been a one he'd wanted to keep. While there had been women who would have stayed with him, he didn't believe any such woman would want a man like him ... permanent.

Since he'd never wanted to keep one of them, it had never mattered. This one, this Wallis Witherspoon could be different. He might want to keep her.

How could he think something like that this soon?

He frowned his narrowed eyes into the blustering wind and he could smell the rain coming. He considered the woman against his back. She had spunk. She'd been trapped in a car for three days, and she'd worried about the puma and the kits. She hadn't whined or complained or come apart, even once.

It was an earnest storm by the time they reached the sheltered, tacky line shack down a roll of land surrounded by mesquites with one large oak. He dismounted, then lifted her down off Frankenstein. Then he led the horse to the better three-sided shed in back. There he unsaddled the horse, wiped him down, forked down hay and put up the token barrier to keep the horse in the shelter.

Leo stayed in the shed.

As the couple walked to the shack, Wallis considered it. Shack was what it really was. Unpainted. Raw. Tacky. She chuffed a laugh. "Any port in a storm?" She gestured toward the shack.

He looked at it to see it from her point of view. He defended it logically. "It's got a good roof. It's snug. You'll apologize when you've sheltered here a while."

"A...while?"

In his careful way, Clint told her, "This will be at least a three-day gully washer. It does just that. All the gullies will be filled and running. The wind will blow all the pecans down, and we'll have pecan hunts for the cooks to make tasty pies and fruitcakes and Christmas cookies. Relax. You'll be able to move around and cook and—"

She gently tasted the word. "Cook?"

The door wasn't locked. He allowed her to wait as he went inside and looked around the approximately eighteen-by-eighteen-foot interior. No one or no creature was there. He asked, "Can't you cook?"

She went into the storm-darkened room. It was one room. No bathroom? She replied automatically, "No. I can't cook at all well."

He sighed rather too well and assured her, "I'll mark that on the debit side."

"Debit?" She was surprised he knew such a word.

"Debit is a no-no on the place. You avoid debits."

She looked around. "Yeah. Probably. There *is* more room here than in the station wagon." She was conceding a rather grudging compliment.

Clint considered her. Never in his life had anything confined him. And he began to appreciate the three days that she'd been a woman alone in a cramped space.

That was a beginning. She had been a woman, alone. "Why were you alone?"

"I don't need anyone holding my hand."

He was so startled by her statement that the laugh lines around his eyes were pale. She could stand there in his jacket, in a sheltered place he'd taken her, and say such? He and Leo had just spent that very day in a rescue of her and she claimed—? Women!

But he looked at the waterlogged, shivering female and his heart was touched by her bravado...and her femininity. He knew how to get her warm. "I'll build a fire, and you can get out of those wet clothes."

"Good. I'm frozen."

He went about building the fire efficiently. Closer to the sink, to one side, in the middle of the room was an iron stove with a flat top on which to cook. The pipe went out through the roof. There was wood handy, restocked by the last ones who'd harbored there.

"Is there anyone you need to contact?" He watched her with more interest than he knew.

And she replied, "Not yet."

He didn't ask her to spread her reply out for its meaning.

There were no dishes in the sink. Leaving the place tidy was a harsh rule.

While the cabin had no frills, at all, it was well stocked. There were four bunks and four windows. The two upper bunk beds folded up out of the way and were hooked to the wall.

The pillows were on the bottom, mattressed benches, which would serve for lounging or sitting or daytime snoozes. Under the bottom bunks were storage bins. Wallis looked. In them, there were blankets, sheets and towels.

There was a wooden table and four chairs. Under one window was a hand pump into a zinc sink. Along that wall were sideboards and cupboards.

There was a stack of old newspapers and magazines. The stove was cleared out already, so the last people there had been quite tidy.

Clint escorted her to check out the privy before leaving her there. She was surprised to find the privy was clean.

She returned to the shack to find Clint's fire was cheerily crackling in the iron stove.

From one cupboard, he took out some clean long johns and a shirt. He gave those to Wallis as he said, "I'll turn my back. Get out of those wet things, and give me my jacket. I'll hang it up here so's it can dry."

Then she noted the wire strung high across the room from the door to the other side and over the stove. And she thought, of course, only lousy weather would drive men into such a place, and they'd probably be wet. Ergo, a line for drying and clean basics available. How smart.

He'd put his boots the right distance from the stove, but he hung her tennies over the stove with clothespins. Then he said, "Give me your things as you take them off." He moved over by the door and stood with his back to her.

She told him, "They need washing."

"I'll carry them outside to the line and let the rain do it."

"Please."

And with her word, he smiled inside him. She was a mannered lady. With his back to her disrobing by the crackling stove, he listened to every sound she made.

She threw the discarded clothing past him on the floor. He watched from the sides of his eyes as he picked them up. She'd had those panties next to her. And peripherally he saw her bending over, putting her foot into the leg of the long johns. She was something.

She was concentrating on what she was doing. She was earnest, trusting . . . of *him!* She assumed since his back was to her that he wasn't watching. Her naked body boggled him. When had a woman last boggled him? Excited, sure, but boggled? He'd been about, what? Twelve?

He stood up, holding her clothing in his big hands, his back was still to her. He appeared to be straightening the clothes, but he was watching her. She was turned away, pulling on the smallest size of cotton long johns he'd been able to find. Over the long johns, she shrugged into a large, heavy cotton shirt that hung down past her knees.

He almost asked if she wanted a towel, but he stopped himself in time and asked, "You dressed?"

"Yes."

He turned, and she was so little and helpless looking in that oversize collection of men's clothing that he smiled at her. "Want a towel?"

"Please."

He found a towel in the storage area under one bunk and handed it to her. "There's a regular supply crew that comes around the line camps and puts in food and clean towels and stuff."

"I'm glad. Just to be dry. This fire is wonderful. Thank you."

And he smiled.

Three

————

Clint put on his Stetson and took Wallis's clothes outside. He was back inside almost immediately.

She inquired, "Did you just pitch my clothes on the dump heap?"

He grinned at her as he hung his Stetson on one of the pegs by the door and replied, "No. I really did hang them up. The line is from the corner of the shack there—" he pointed to the front right corner "—to the tree on out thataway." And he wiped his feet on the rug by the door.

"Tree?" she questioned dubiously.

He sat on one of the chairs around the table and leaned the chair back to balance it on two back legs. He was ready to talk. "The pincher clothespins are handily left on the wire line, and we just put clothes on it. Everybody knows the line's there because it's the same way at every line shack. That way, nobody gets his neck caught running around the shack.''

''Why...would anyone be running around the shack?''

''Lose at cards? Win? Not clean their plates? See a woman escape? Criticize the cook?''

She sat down across from him and folded her hands on the table as she said, ''Uhh...''

He hastened to explain, ''Women are forbidden in the shacks?'' That was a do-you-understand, questioning statement. ''Strictly forbidden. If anybody comes along while we're here, you'll have to sneak through the far window and stay in the shed.''

She slowly put her head all the way back and brought it down once to confirm that direction. ''Right.''

''It's the rule.''

She tilted her head back and looked at him down her nose. ''I'll find an arbitrator, and we'll just see who has to stay in the shed.''

He was disgusted and explained with patient slowness, ''A cranky woman has to walk very careful, or a man knows what she's like. A really smart woman would inquire which window is closest to the shed.'' He said window as win-da.

''Which one is closest?''

''That one, right there.'' He pointed.

''Over the sink?'' she exclaimed in disbelief. Then she lectured in rejection, ''It would be tacky of me to climb up in the sink in order to get out that window. My bare feet have been walking on this...floor.''

With stunned surprise, he proclaimed, ''You're... couth!''

She preened and turned her head in elaborate show-offiness before she replied, ''Naturally.''

He bragged on her. "You've hidden it pretty good."
She grinned and then shared the laugh.

"I'm sorry I didn't think to get you some socks." He
got up and sorted through the several pairs rolled up in
the underwear drawer. "Try these. They're the smallest I can find."

The socks were thick and wonderful on her bare, cold
feet. She said, "Thank you." Then she asked, "Aren't
you going to offer me something to eat?"

"Peacock brains?"

"That's . . . tongues," she corrected with gentle tact.

He considered her correction. "Whose?" he asked.

"You're supposed to serve a lady peacock tongues,
not their brains."

"Well, I'll be a— I've always thought it was brains,
because a lady eats so delicate and all."

"The tongues," she reiterated, but she went on and
explained further, "Because peacocks are shrill. And
ladies need the encouragement to speak up."

He laughed so hard that he had to put the chair's
front legs back on the floor, but his eyes brimmed humor and he shared that with the wicked Wallis Witherspoon.

She said prissily, "It would behoove you to feed me
before I faint."

He started to rise, then sat back down and said, "I
know how to give mouth-to-mouth."

"I can't bully my way into your kitchen and feed
myself without permission."

Then he remembered that she hadn't eaten for some
time. "Yes. I give the permission, but I'd be glad to fix
you something." He went to a small section of the cupboards and removed a can of beans, one of tomatoes,
one of corn and a bottle of chili pepper.

She rose and said, "Allow me."

"Do you know how to make tortillas?"

"No."

He instructed, "I'll do those. You put these together, there's olive oil, there, and the skillet is there, the rice is there and so are the beans."

"I'm not sure my stomach can handle chili."

"When did you last eat?"

"This morning."

Clint said, "Surely to goodness, if you ate just this morning, you can handle a little chili?"

"I've *had* TEXAS chili. I know how potent it can be."

"Well, here, you're in full control. Just don't put so much chili pepper on yours."

"Yes."

She got out the skillet and put an oil coating in it. She put the skillet on the stove. She looked at Clint, who was down the kitchen side, sprinkling flour on the dusty counter. She suggested, "Perhaps the counter should be washed first?"

That apparently surprised him. He said, "Wet counters make the tortillas stick."

"How about dusting it?"

He frowned at her and accused, "You're picky."

"Yes."

"Well, I'll just have to take that under advisement."

"Do that."

He wiped the counter with a paper towel and threw the towel into the stove. Then he began to mix water into the cornmeal.

She looked for a can opener until he took out his knife and opened all the cans with a sawing blade. The sound of it was a lot like fingernails on a blackboard.

She shivered and covered her ears, so he said, "You're a nuisance. You don't know how to do anything."

She added, "But cook normally."

He made a disbelieving sound and went back to fixing tortillas.

She tasted the mixture discreetly. Then she inquired, "Do you have butter?"

He exclaimed in shock, "Butter. You mean from . . . cows?"

"Yes."

"The only cows we have feed mavericks. The cows are wild, unreasonable and unmilkable."

"You just eat the tortillas unadorned?"

"Yep. We do everything thataway. No frills. Basic food, fermented wines and vegetables like our sex—raw."

She predicted, "Someday you will become civilized."

"I don't see no reason for it."

"Sometime, you should sample civilization."

"I have. It's lacking."

And she laughed.

The trouble was, she'd hit a nerve in him. He knew he wasn't smooth or civilized, and he felt the lack of it with her. He'd always been confident he was the best. Now she'd made him unsure.

He was bandying around and seemingly rougher than he really was because he couldn't be smooth enough. Therefore, he appeared to be clowning, when he was really pretty much the way he was acting.

The shack was getting warmer, and she was relaxing. He was tightening. His movements were rather elaborately casual.

She was searching the cabinet for condiments and spices. The supply consisted of salt, pepper and chili powder.

She delicately sautéed the varied collection from cans, adding it to the onions and rice. He moved her pan over and began to toast the tortillas on the end of the stove-top.

Keeping an eye on the tortillas, he got glasses from the cupboard and poured wine from a big brown earthen jug. Then he put on a pot of coffee.

He lifted one glass and handed it to her as she turned tortillas.

But as he reached to get the other glass, she said, "I don't think I should have anything to drink that's alcoholic. I haven't had solid food all day. I might get silly."

He thought: Good. But with some talent, he looked concerned. "Put your glass on the table and drink the wine with your meal. Beans are notorious for countering alcohol." His face was earnest and believable.

She *tsked* once and said, "You do try."

He smiled so sweetly, but his laughter rumbled around inside him. He was gonna git'er.

He put a kerosene lamp on the table and lighted it. That's when Wallis realized it was getting dark. Outside, the wind was strong and the rain was pelting, splatting against the windows.

When it thundered, the shack trembled and the dishes jiggled with little sounds.

She commented, "The storm's getting worse."

Since it was exactly as it had been since it had arrived, his attention was alerted. She'd been so tense that she'd only been conscious of him. She'd been wary of him.

Did Clint reassure her? No. He said pleasantly, "I hope you brought your knitting. With the runoff from this storm, we could be here for several days."

"I've already noticed the cards."

"Do you play honeymoon bridge?" He asked that with an innocent, eyebrow-lifting interest.

"I can play any card game there is."

He was a-*ghast!* "Strip poker?" He put his hand on his chest and drew back a step in rather too elaborate shock.

Prissily, she pronounced, "Plain...poker."

"At a penny a bump?"

"I'll consult my banker."

"You don't have a penny on you. I've already frisked you. How are you going to bet? Kisses?"

She saw his eyes were hot. Wait a minute, here, what was she getting into? She said, "I play double solitaire."

"We bet."

"On solitaire?" She was scoffing.

"Who's out of cards first, wins."

She made the rules. "We play for the skill."

"I have to see your hands and rings."

She sassily put down her stirring spoon and held out her hands as she said, "No rings."

He pushed softly, "No ties?"

Snootily she said, "I have a plaid one that—"

But he was serious. He finished his question. "With another man." How revealing that he'd ask such a question on such short acquaintance. What was he doing inquiring, this soon?

She moved rather casually and replied, "Not really."

"Some guy interested?"

She repeated the two words, "Not really."

"Does he know you say he's not really interested? How big is he?"

"He couldn't match you."

Clint licked his smile. He was sure that no man could. Not even his boss Lemon Covington. Lemon's trouble was that he was a gentleman, while Clint Terrell was not.

He held Wallis's chair as she was seated. He'd learned that from watching Lemon. And she sat there in someone's cotton long johns and someone else's great shirt and wearing socks that were too big. Her black hair was dry and curling around her head in a careless, marvelous, finger-combed mass. Her face was serene and her eyes confident.

She affected him strongly. His gaze on her was possessive. His breathing was carefully casual. He was a typical stalker. He knew how to fool game. Ah, but she wasn't something a man hunted. She needed courting.

She'd already tasted the rice-bean-vegetable combination, and now she tasted the tortillas. They were thicker than commercial ones, but they were simply delicious. And the wine was excellent.

Clint was a good communicator. His slow, sorted words questioned and teased, and he laughed and told incidents where he was the fool or fooled or the patsy. He made her laugh so hard.

He was curious about her searching for weeds, and she wanted to know why he was annoying the cattle by insisting they obey his rules.

They were good companions. She listened and chatted and responded with tales of her own, and the storm raged outside in such a way it seemed they'd be trapped forever in the shack.

She looked around, seeing the shack differently. It was well made and quite comfortable. The stove was perfect, the place was carefully planned to accommodate more than just two people, and it was efficient.

He took a plate out to Leo and came back to shake water from his Stetson and return it to one of the pegs by the door. He shed his jacket to put it back on the high line to dry again. Then he added more wood to the stove and took off his vest and boots.

She had cleared the table and washed the dishes. He came and said softly, "You're a good companion."

She laughed, "Because I do dishes."

He said in a husky voice, "Ladies always kiss their rescuer. You haven't kissed me."

She would have sassed something in reply, but he was earnest. The squint lines were again white. She said, "I did thank you several times. You planned it perfectly. Have you rescued very many people?" She was busy with wiping the table.

He took her arm and said, "Let's go to bed."

She replied pleasantly, "You must be exhausted. It is late. Go ahead and sleep. I'll watch."

"You gotta be tired. Come stretch out here on this bunk." He put the pillows side by side down on the bottom bunk on the right side of the room. From the chest, he got out a covering blanket.

She noted it was about a three-quarters bed, wide enough and long enough for a man to be comfortable. She told him seriously, "You forget I was confined for three days. I'm restless. It's marvelous to move around."

He promised, "I'll give you exercise."

"No. Thanks, anyway."

He coaxed, "You'd like it."

"So I hear."

That stopped him as he frowned, "You . . . don't?"

"No." She sat at the table and shuffled the cards.

"Come on, don't be a holdout. Loosen up and enjoy your adventure . . . with me."

"You don't get pregnant. I could."

He grinned wickedly. "It just so happens I have some condoms with me in my saddlebag. When I fed Leo, I got a couple."

She didn't look at him, but she inquired rather sparsely, "That work very often?"

"I've never had to ask twice."

"Wow." She said it with no emphasis at *all* and dealt out hands for double solitaire. "You must really be a stud. You don't need to experience me. Go out to the shed and sleep with the other animals."

Was he offended? No. He complained. "My eyes'll bulge and I'll get restless."

She looked at her hand. "Leo will protect me." She lay down the hand and said, "Gin."

"Leo's my dog. He'll do as I say."

"You might be surprised. Are you going to play?"

"I'm sure as hell trying."

She refused playing his game. "Why should I? You could be riddled with all the various diseases, plus the fatal one."

"I'm careful." He was deadly serious.

"So am I. No."

He threw in the ringer, "I saved your life."

"That puma mother was starving. She would have had to leave and find food so that she and her kittens could survive. I had enough water for a month. I knew what I was doing."

"And now you're in a cabin in a storm that'll last a couple-a days, the river's wild and you're with a needy man that's bigger'n you."

She took up the cards she'd dealt him and spread them and tidied them as to suits. She said absently, "Leo will protect me."

"Not all the time. He has to go outside to—"

So she was blunt. "Rape? Perhaps. But then you're vulnerable. You have to sleep some time. I'd probably castrate you." She said that quite calmly as she examined the cards.

"You wouldn't. You couldn't. You save flowers. You'd save me. Come on. Let's. It's nice. You'll like it. You'll like it so much, you'll be at my body for the rest of the time we're here."

She put his cards down and picked up her own. She said, "I know nothing about you at all, except that Leo can direct you to help something. You thought I was a valuable beef, instead of a nothing woman."

Earnestly he assured her, "You're something. Really something."

She scoffed impatiently, "You're selling." She looked at him levelly. "Since I know what's in your hand—" she wasn't really talking about cards "—perhaps you'd like me to redeal?"

He took a very long, slow breath, exhaled in disgust and replied, "I'll deal."

So they were in a hot and heavy game and quarreling hilariously, competitively, when Clint heard someone in the shed.

He got up instantly and blew out the lamp. In the stone dark, they listened.

One voice called, "Hey, the house, we—"

Another voice corrected, "It's a shack."

"Hey, the shack. It's George and Mike and Poopsi."

Clint said a muttered sentence that would have tightly curled her ducktailed hair if she'd heard. But he only muttered as he went to the door. He yelled, "Go on home!"

The voice had to wait for the thunder to pass before it said, "Now that's not hospitable, a-tall. What're you—"

A lower voice asked, "You got a *woman* here?"

And a rough voice chided, "Now, Clint, you know you're not supposed to ruin our morals thataway."

Their laughter was silly and funny as they teased, coming up to the front and only door.

Seeing the clothes on the line, one said, "Who's the squirt that wears— Clint? You really got a woman here? While we've been working our tails off with those walking steaks, have you been here f—"

"Shut up."

"Boy, are you testy! What's going on?"

Clint lighted the lamp. He was standing, the three arrivals were crowding into the doorway, and Wallis was sitting at the table, holding cards, looking at them.

They gasped and went speechless. They stared.

Clint growled. "Mind your manners."

All three took off their hats.

That was the extent of manners?

One said, "Company! Can she cook?"

The other two stared, stricken, curious, envious, as Clint growled, "Behave."

They moved a little and looked at their feet. They wiped them in turns on the old rug at the door, which was there for that purpose.

Clint wondered if they'd ever bothered to stop and wipe their boots off before then. It was their way of behaving. Clint sighed in his mind and thought that stubborn woman would have to sleep with him now—there were only four bunks and five people. He smiled at the intruders and asked, "Have you had supper?"

"Jerky."

It was easier to say than pemmican. They were staring at Wallis.

She was unflappable.

Clint said, "This is Mike, that one's George and he's LeRoy."

She figured out LeRoy was the one they'd called Poopsi.

George asked, "What's your name, honey?"

Clint replied, "You don't have to know."

Mike inquired, "Oh, you staked her out?"

But it was young, skinny LeRoy who said, "Leave her be."

Wallis asked Clint, "Shall I fix something for them?"

"They can do it."

George suggested, "A chocolate cake with white icing."

She laughed.

They laughed unduly.

She said, "There isn't even a can opener here. There are no cake mixes."

Mike was appalled, "You need a *mix?*"

She replied, "Yep."

LeRoy said, "There's only four bunks. You can share mine."

He'd seemed so kind and fragile!

Clint shifted and his head came forward a trifle.

Wallis said, "You can sleep with Clint."

That made George and Mike laugh.

Clint was watching the men. LeRoy looked at Wallis and shook his head. He said, ''Clint doesn't like males.'' Then LeRoy said, ''You got a stubborn, narrow-minded woman there, Clint, and you ought to reconsider her.''

''Shut up.''

They were terrified in a really hammy manner, and she laughed. The three visitors loved it and laughed with her.

Clint was disgusted. ''You have no idea what you've started. You've laughed, and they think you think they're clever. Now we'll hear lousy jokes and sly jokes all night long.''

Mike said, ''He's jealous.''

It didn't take much for Wallis to understand that Clint was hostile because now *he* would have to behave himself.

That amused Wallis most of all.

She did nothing. She sat and listened, and they played to her with asides and jokes and plays on words. Hilariously awful.

Clint only monitored their language. He would smile because they were funny. He sat, leaning the chair on the back two legs, and he listened.

The three intruders cooked, and they were practiced in cooperating and getting it done. They had about what Clint and Wallis had eaten, and they talked the whole time. When did they chew?

They were tired and wet. The day had been an irritation and the cattle ornery. The horses were balky. Buck had been thrown and broke an arm. They'd had to splint it and take him to an opening where he could be fetched by the plane. The threat of the storm had made the pickup really hairy.

Then, they had to keep his horse from following the plane as it took off. It had been a bitc—rough day. And that gully washer! They'd been high enough to be safe. But they saw a deer caught in it swirl away downstream.

They had to go to bed because they had to get up at midnight and relieve the guys coping with the beasts out in that wild night. They just wanted to get dry and warm.

They warned Wallis not to peek—endlessly—as they changed clothes. They took those discarded ones, squeezed them out in the sink and hung the wrung clothes on the high line.

They did all that without even thinking about it. So automatically that Wallis wondered how many times they'd been that tired, that wet and that funny.

They shook down the stove, added logs, washed their dishes and talked the entire time.

She had to go to the privy. Her shoes were just about dry, and they took her shoes down from the wire. Then they argued who would get to help her into her shoes. They argued while she was putting them on.

The three gave her advice. "Wear Clint's hat and go naked. When you come back—"

Young LeRoy yelled, "We'll get you dry!"

The whole time they teased Wallis, they were eyeing Clint as they tried to get every wicked thing said before he blew.

Clint made a very serious sound.

"Who're you going to sleep with, honey? Two of us can't sleep together because we're just too big. But a little girl like you has a good choice. We're clean and rainwashed. You won't choke being in be—"

Clint said, "Cut it out."

"What a stickler. George, did you ever in this world dream that *Clinton* Terrell would be picky and snotty about what was said to a woman?"

George sighed hugely. "It comes on all of us, sooner or later."

Thoughtfully, LeRoy mentioned, "Good song title."

Mike explained, "LeRoy's our next Eddy Raven. Ever heard Raven's 'I've Got Mexico'? Man. We all suffer."

Clint suggested, "Get to bed."

"Who—"

Clint decided it. "LeRoy, you go to the barn. There're five good horses out yonder that need comforting."

LeRoy took a deep breath. "I'm always the privileged one."

They ruffled his hair and slapped his shoulders and got him out of the shack.

Wallis said, "Since LeRoy will see to the horses, Leo can come inside."

There was no way they could get around that. Clint did try. "He's an outside dog."

"Have you ever given him the chance?"

"You'll ruin him." Clint considered that Leo was always inside at Lemon's house. In his slow, careful choosing of words, he assured her, "A herd dog like Leo would be restless inside here. The men need their sleep."

The two obediently bobbed their heads in serious agreement.

Wallis went to the door and called, "Leo!"

He was there before she'd finished the *o*. He was that fast.

She took a clean towel and wiped off the sprinkle of raindrops from his yellow coat. He loved it.

The men watched sour faced.

Clint told them to get to bed. And they did do that.

The two men were so tired, there was nothing for the other two to do but also go to bed.

So Wallis said, "I have dibs on the bottom bunk."

Well, there was no way, at all, that Clint was going to allow some other man to sleep closer to Wallis than he did. But he did try. "I need to know exactly where you are."

"I'll be in this bunk."

It galled Clint. And he shot commanding stares at the two alert and watching hands. He said, "The upper bunk is just a tad narrower than the bottom one."

"So." She was courteous, allowing him to explain.

"I'm bigger'n you."

"Then arm wrestle Mike for the bottom one across the room."

And without explaining, Clint said, "No."

She stated her stand, "I want the bottom bunk."

"Sounds logical to me, how about you?" Mike turned with interest to George.

"I don't have no trouble with her wanting the bottom bunk."

So Clint said, "Okay." Whatever that meant.

The two men accepted that Clint was telling them to get to sleep.

Wallis was gracious. "I'll get to bed after you get up there. You'll need to step on the side of my bed to get to yours."

He looked at her levelly and didn't say anything. He was checking her out to see if she was really magic. And damn it to hell, she was.

So Clint slept in the bunk above Wallis—and Leo slept with her. She said, "Leo, come." Then she moved back against the wall.

The dog smiled and stepped up carefully, arranging his bulk, trying to minimize himself just like any male with a female. He curled down and was careful.

The other two men slept almost immediately. Wallis settled down and was silent. The damned dog snored.

Clint lay awake and wondered what was happening to him.

Four

It was about six the next morning when Wallis stretched and yawned. There was dead silence. She opened her eyes and found Leo's big head resting on her stomach. She took his head between her hands and said softly, "You're getting pushy, do you realize that? And you have more than your half of the—"

She looked beyond the dog and saw five men absolutely fascinated! They were watching her. They were clean and tidy, and they were eating silently.

It had been the smell of coffee that had awakened her. She said, "Good morning."

They all replied as if triggered simultaneously or directed by a conductor's wand. She smiled, and they all smiled back, as if each was the sole recipient of her smile. What an ego trip!

His face gentle, Clint brought her a cup of coffee and

put another pillow under her shoulders as she moved to accept the cup.

One male voice cautioned with soft, compassionate chiding, "You're gonna spoil her rotten, you do that."

Another asked gently, "That my shirt? I'll never get it to behave after it being on her thataway."

And in a low voice, the third questioned, "Yours? Bullsh—uh—I don't believe it is. I think it might be the one I used to wear."

Clint said, "It's mine."

"Well, sh-ucks. I thought it was my lucky shirt. I sure need it back. I've got to go out in this weather and deal with them beeves that don't want to do nothing my way. It was nice of you to warm it for me before I had to go out into this—"

Clint told Leo, "Come on, boy. Heaven's over."

The men all chortled very quietly and glanced at each other.

She asked, "Did you just come in for breakfast?"

And one of the shaking heads replied before anyone else got started. "We come in just after midnight? Clint said he'd kill us if we made any sound at all. You didn't hear us, so we did survive."

She laughed.

There, she'd done it again! She laughed, and they all became comedians to entertain her and get her to look at them. What a bunch of hams.

All but one.

He was younger than Clint's thirty-eight years. He sat wickedly sprawling, and he said not a word. He'd look at Clint and then he'd look at Wallis. He looked at her longer, but his imagination was in overdrive.

Leo went out the door.

"Did he get breakfast?" she asked.

And three replied, "Yeah...that rotten dog... 'course."

And the hooded-eyed, sprawling man said, "We saved you some pancakes."

Clint's head turned slowly and he just looked at the speaker, who ignored Clint.

Wallis was aware of the bandying needling and she didn't encourage it at all. She said, "The coffee is perfect."

An older man beamed. "It'll grow hair on your chest."

That got some knee slappings and chortling.

She let it pass.

The oldest one asked, "How come you got such a beauty? The old lady I rescued, let's see, it's been about seven years ago now, no, it was before the Pill was here, so it had to be about nine years ago and she—"

One of his party said, "Get on with it, Ed, for God's sake. He can make a two-liner into three books."

"She was the most cantankerous woman! She was a *horror,* I swear to tell you. Talk! It poured out of her mouth with it *closed!* I never seen nothing to match her."

"Well, Meg Gilly could beat her. I was in a blizzard in '86 with that woman and my ears still ain't right. They's echoing words. She had conversation backed up ten mile!"

But there was rebuttal. A scrawny one put in, "Women ain't as bad as men, jawing's not too bad. Remember Jess Effingham? I got him out of his well. I had to dig him out and mad! He had a real fit, he did! He made me clean it all up and redo the well. I never went back there for water."

They never slowed down eating, but they all talked. They laughed at odd times and hushed a talker now and again.

Wallis tried to figure out why.

Clint was lazily watching the men in an extremely dangerous manner.

The visitors knew that. And it pleased them all. They didn't have much else for entertainment, so this was the way they passed the time, needling, taunting, pushing, working, helping, saving and struggling.

She changed the subject. "How could you be so quiet that I didn't waken?"

"Clint threatened us with such graphic—such terrible things that we daren't say a word or make a sound. He scares us."

She laughed.

And the visitors laughed along with her.

Clint didn't change expression. He said, "They're waiting for you guys to relieve them."

"We're on our way." The oldest man got up, and then looked back as if he'd just thought of it. "I hear tell you got yourself a good horse since Buck was flown to the hospital. All that fuss over a little broken arm! I don't know what the world's coming to. But since you got a horse, you can come—"

"Yeah! It'd be something different for you. Come with us!"

Clint said, "No."

Wallis put in easily, "I'm not a horse rider."

"Oh? Then what do you ride?"

"Cars, trains and planes."

"One of those." The sprawled man growled.

Wallis was particularly aware that her name hadn't been given, either. Clint hadn't told the men last night, and he very obviously hadn't told these men, this morning. She wondered why.

And none had inquired.

The older man said, "Brace yourself, you'll be getting a new shift in here when we get to the herd."

"Aren't you moving?" Clint asked.

"Oh, sure, but the crew coming in will catch up. They've had a long, wet night."

Clint said, "Yeah."

They all put their hats on, in order to take them off and tip them at her. She smiled and lifted a hand to acknowledge that.

She heard one say to Clint, "All's we can give you is about a half hour. That time en—"

And Clint took his arm in a hard hand.

All innocence, the man whispered in a fake manner, "I was just trying to help out."

And through his teeth, Clint said, "Out."

As one went out the door, he grumbled, "Got a burr under his tail." But humor laced the words.

Another began, "She'll—" Something stopped his words.

Clint followed them outside and his voice was a low growl.

So Wallis took that opportunity to get her sneakers off the high wire. That was when she noted that someone, probably Clint, had brought her rainwashed clothes inside and hung them on the high wire. That was very thoughtful.

She put the sneakers on and peeked out the window. Clint was walking through the downpour with the silent men to the shed where the horses were. She went out to the privy. It was still neat and orderly.

She returned to the shack and no one was there. She combed her wildly free hair and ate some dried apricots from the open box on the table.

When Clint came back inside, Leo wasn't with him. Clint closed the door and looked at Wallis.

She said, "Rather a cheerfully raunchy bunch."

"I couldn't control them."

"They weren't that bad. They were teasing you to see if they could ruffle your feathers."

He was serious. "A guest ought to be treated better. I apologize for them."

"They meant no harm." She sipped her second cup of coffee.

He wanted to settle her fears. "If I hadn't of been here to take their teasing, they'd of been dumb."

"Stupid or silent?"

He gestured with one hand to expand the few words. "Not saying nothing."

"They work hard."

He said seriously, "I'm glad you know that. They're good men. They just never really see your kind of woman, and they get—uh—stimulated? I'm trying to find another word for excited."

"Stimulated is a good word."

Clint gestured awkwardly with both hands. "They get a little horny. They talk different. Naw. They talk the same. All our talk's that way. We have a hard time when a woman's around. Especially if she's pretty, like you."

"Thank you."

"Why?"

"You called me pretty."

"Hell, woman, you know that."

"But you told me."

"Nobody's ever said that to you before now? Now who's foolin' who?"

She said seriously, "I like hearing you say it."

"You coming on to me?"

She was impatient. "No."

"Then you be careful."

She questioned with some disbelief, "Just thanking you for saying—"

And he turned on her with some annoyance, "Take it easy on me, woman. Don't push for my attention. I'll *give* it! And from what you've said, you don't want it."

She replied logically, "I met you just yesterday."

"So?"

She frowned at him. "Today is too...sudden for me. So was last night."

"How long does it take you?"

That made her indignant. "I don't know."

Disgruntled, he walked to a window as he accused, "You want me to pant after you and wait and hurt."

"No."

He turned on her and asked intensely, "Then *what?*"

Her temper rising, she retorted, "I have no idea. But I would need to know the kind of man you are, and whether I would want to do something...like... something that..."

He put both hands into his thick hair and groaned, "God save a man from a virgin."

"Why?"

"It takes too long."

She huffed and couldn't find words.

He told her with impatience, "Come eat. I'll take you over to our place, and we can get a car for you."

After a thoughtful, rather sorrowful pause, she commented, "I can't believe mine's gone."

"Yes."

Pensively, she said, "I wonder where it is."

He put pancakes on a plate for her. "Even if we could find it, I doubt your car'll ever work again. It's probably battered and still rolling down the riverbed with the trees and junk the gully washer picked up."

"It was stuck. And it was in that little cove." She poured syrup on the pancakes.

He elaborated, "It was stuck on a rock. You couldn't rock it off. The flood would've lifted it right off and carried it away. The power of the river is something."

And she thought of his power. His control of horse and dog . . . and men.

She lifted a forkful of pancake from her plate as she inquired courteously, "Do you bed women the first twenty-four hours all the time?"

He looked at her in a slow, rather cold way and asked, "That your business?"

"It just surprises me that you'd expect me to jump into bed with you when I've just met you."

"You're a cold woman."

"How can you be so careless of yourself? What do you know about me? I could be riddled with all the terrible diseases and—"

"Are you?"

She looked at him with great interest and some censure. "You'd take my word?"

"You look honest."

"As I understand it, so did Lucrezia Borgia."

"I haven't run acrost her."

"She poisoned people."

"Oh." And he gave up. She knew things he didn't know and she would dust them off every time they disagreed. He would feel—less than he was.

He straightened to his height and looked around like the throwback he was. All that was wrong was that he was in the wrong century. He went outside and took out the damned communicator and said, "This is Clint."

A male voice said, "Huh?"

Then Lemon's woman, Renata, said, "You all okay?"

Typically, since it was his contact, he ignored her question and asked his own. "How's Buck?"

"Very comfortable. You know those nurses over at the hospital? He thinks he's in—uh—hog heaven? He's also on a narcotic—uh—easer?" Renata had been raised in a very sheltered manner. She was struggling to adjust to the different environment of Cactus Ridge.

And Clint's eyes narrowed. If that mouse Renata could bring herself to fit in, so could this terror inside the shack. It wasn't him who needed the adjusting to her, it was the other way around.

Then he looked at the gadget in his hand that allowed Lemon to horn in on his people any time at all. It was a newfangled gadget . . . and Clint Terrell was using it.

He said to Lemon's love, "We might be another day or so. She's really worn. The crews have been nice to her." He said that so they didn't sound alone. "They haven't been as raunchy as usual."

Renata laughed.

See? She could laugh at the men's crudeness. She was adjusting.

Clint said the closing word gently and shut the damned gadget off.

It was still raining in blustering gusts. He smiled. He could keep her there at least another night. At noon, the last of the men would be gone. The cattle were being moved so that the fragile, saturated ground wasn't harmed by their hooves. They would move on. She would be alone with him.

He stood in that basic place and lifted his head to look at the untamed, windblown, storm-tossed relentless mesquites. Of all the useless things, the mesquite was about at the top of the list.

They were too short to be climbed for safety. They couldn't be used to hang a man . . . his feet would drag on the ground. They were knurled, thorny and mean. No use at all. Of course, the beans were sweet and made one hell of a hair-lifting liquor.

Any attempt to destroy the trees was a useless effort. TEXANS had finally cut them down and burned them. It was hard work and the smoke polluted the air. The trees won by sheer numbers. So TEXANS cut up the wood and sold it around the country as perfect fuel for cooking on an outside grill. He smiled. A modern adjustment.

Grudgingly, Clint considered whether that woman was worth his trying to adjust to her way of doing things. That meant waiting.

Sourly, he considered all the women who'd turned him down like she was trying to do. And he couldn't remember very many. He probably hadn't known them well enough *to* remember them. Was that right? How come he'd never considered how many had rejected him before then?

It was because then he'd only been concerned with himself? That was sobering. He'd had no family. He'd taken care of himself for a long, long time. His last adult kinsman had died when he was eleven. That's when he'd come to Lemon's family. The cattlemen had given him room and raised him with their rules.

Why would this particular woman make him look at his life? Hell. She might as well know him as he really was, no frills. No lies. Just him.

He went inside and said, "Need clean clothes? If you're quick, you can run out and rinse off in the rain."

"I smell better today than I have in some time. I'd been two additional days without a bath before I got stuck!" She grinned.

Damn. She looked perfect. Why did he want to hide his flaws with this woman? How could he be honest about himself... with her? She'd just disappear without ever having really considered him.

To consider him? Why did he want her to do that? Why her?

He asked, "Are you hiding your flaws from me?"

"I hope not."

"What's that mean?"

"I wouldn't fool you."

"I'm trying to be honest with you."

"Blunt. That's what you've been."

He frowned. "How do you figure that?"

"You aren't trying to impress me, nor are you trying to lure me."

His voice became gentle in the oddest way. "You want to be... lured?"

"Not yet."

He gasped. He actually did. He walked around a little and rubbed his stomach up by his ribs and his body was intense.

She was puzzled by his reaction. She asked carefully, "What did I say?"

"It was the 'not yet' that hooked into me."

She was surprised by him. "How could my refusal affect you? I do mean that I'm not about to jump into the sack with you."

"You're saying, maybe later?"

"I don't know you at all. Why would I suggest such a thing?"

"I think maybe we're on two levels."

"Agreed."

He began to take off his shirt, and she gasped.

He looked at her blankly and realized she'd pulled back. He looked at his body. No woman had ever pulled back from seeing him. What was wrong?

Her eyes were big as saucers. She was afraid of him? He frowned at her. "I'm changing clothes."

"Oh."

He smiled just a bit. "Disappointed?"

"I was trying to remember the karate chops."

And he laughed. "I probably shouldn't tell you this, but I'm black belt."

"How vulgar of you."

"What a snippy woman you are."

She came closer to look at him. He was battered. She touched the butterfly tattoo on his arm. "A butterfly?"

"That's how gentle and sweet I am, and how beautiful and loving I can be."

"You probably collect testimonials?"

"Hot dang, what a good idea!"

On the other arm was a coiled rattler. She put a finger on it. It was very beautifully done. Really well done.

He explained, "That's the other side of me."

"I can believe this one more than I can believe that about the butterfly. I've never seen a man further from being a butterfly."

"Just shows how closed your life's been. I can open you up." He licked away his smile.

"Why tattoos? Were you in the navy?"

"I was on a different kind of ship. Once I was on a piece of ship for almost too long."

"What happened?"

"If you behave improperly, I just might tell you."

He went outside into the rain and shucked the rest of his clothes. She stood back from the window and watched him do that, and she watched as he washed his body. He was simply beautiful.

As he came back inside, she grabbed a magazine from the pile and sat down at the table with her back to the door.

He came in and finished drying as he said, "Sure you don't want a shower?"

"No. Thanks, anyway."

She heard as he pulled on jeans and zipped them.

She casually turned a page, her mind was on "seeing" him.

He came up in back of her and looked over her shoulder, then he reached over and turned the magazine around so that it was seeable for her.

How embarrassing.

He walked away without commenting, but his walk was slow, his back was straight and he walked in a strut.

He found her clean long johns that were somewhat longer, and he found her another shirt. He went out to the shed, and she washed in the sink.

She considered how caring he'd been with her, but she also considered how blatant he was about getting her into his bed.

She heard a shrill whistle and looked outside in time to see the next bunch ride up. They were obviously tired, but they grinned. She could hear their deliberately muffled voices, and she saw that they looked at the shack. There were three of them.

Here they'd go again. And she wondered how much she'd understand of their chatter this time. Maybe it was better that she didn't understand. She'd blush and that would delight them with greater laughs and worse innuendos and more wicked references.

Their visit was as she'd expected. But having eaten, they went to the bunks and flopped down to sleep. They shivered and begged for some kind heart to warm their poor, tired bodies.

Clint whistled for Leo, who came in to great complaining and disgust.

Leo came to Wallis and stood with his tongue hanging out from his big, dog smile.

From the bunks, the men watched and said, "That's the way I feel."

And the others laughed. They, too, wanted to just stand and smile at her.

Wallis squatted down and put her face on Leo's neck and waggled his head. She stood up, and the dog barked.

Wallis laughed, and Leo bounced around like a pup.

She leaned over, and he quietened immediately. He grinned at her, waiting for her to touch him. She said to the dog, "You're a darling."

The men howled like wolves and laughed. Clint took her out of the shack, telling the men to go to sleep.

They said, "After that?"

She didn't understand what was after what. She didn't ask. Leo ran ahead of them to the shed.

She ran after the dog and he bounced around her, barking.

Clint walked normally, as if the weather wasn't that nasty.

At the shed she was playing with the excited dog when Clint came under the shelter. She said, "He's so glad to see us."

Clint growled, "Any male would act thataway if you played with him thataway."

"Phooey. You're just susceptible."

She didn't think the other men were? If she didn't, then she was a woman who was only aware of one man at a time. Had she ever been aware of any other man that way? She was aware of him.

His libido was stimulated by the idea.

She looked up at him and then her glance went over him. "You clean up very nicely." He looked like a barn cat, that chancy and iffy. She looked to see if he had a chewed ear. Surprisingly, he didn't. Now why was that a surprise? He was the kind of man who was in or started brawls for the fun of it.

To distract herself from him, she looked at the horses. The newcomers were standing and very tired. They'd been unsaddled and rubbed down. They were standing on dry hay and under the shelter.

She told Clint softly, "There's only four horses. Where's Buck's horse?"

"I guess the others needed a spare?" That was a questioning statement.

He didn't seem at all surprised. Then she remembered the laughter when he'd walked the last bunch out to the shed. She'd just thought they were telling more jokes.

Had Clint told them to take the horse? "Will your horse carry double all that way?"

"You still have to convince me you need to get back to civilization."

"Uh-oh." She looked over to the shack with the sleeping three inside. They were not choice rescuers. With them, she could be out of the frying pan and into the fire.

Of course, Clint had told her without him the men would be tongue-tied and shy.

He pulled down a bale of hay and set it against the others stacked at the protected end of the shed. He found a blanket and shook it outside the shed, snapping it fairly clean. He spread it on the bale, and Leo immediately jumped up on it.

Disgusted, Clint said, "No, you slob. This is for the lady."

Leo moved over a little.

Wallis laughed and asked, "You two practice this routine?"

"I don't know who all influenced him before me, but somebody ruined a good dog."

She heard the fond teasing in Clint's voice.

"How'd you get him?" She sat on the vacated side of the bale.

Clint shoved Leo off and sat on the other end of the bale. They were pretty close. He put his arm up on the bales in back of them and slouched comfortably. But he was close.

She could hear his breaths. She was aware of his maleness. Her question went unanswered.

To distract herself, she said, "I wonder where that little mother and her babies are by now? I hope they've found as good a place as I."

"She did. They have more than one place. They move around. It's safer thataway."

"She was so distressed."

"Weren't you?"

"I could smell hamburgers. My mouth watered and my stomach growled with shockingly loud sounds. The poor puma probably thought I'd eat her kittens."

He put his hand on her stomach and rubbed it.

He'd shocked her, but her stomach loved his hand there. She said, "Cut that out." Her tone was feeble.

He smiled and said, "Poor tummy. Is it better with the good food I've given you?"

"You make the best tortillas I've ever had. Can you teach me how to do them?"

"I can teach you many things."

"There you go again!"

He was shocked. "What?"

She chided, "You can teach me—many things."

"Besides tortillas, I was talking rope tricks, tracking cattle, coping with weather, telling time by the stars. Did you think it was something else?"

"Well . . ."

"You were right."

And she laughed.

His voice was almost hoarse as he told her, "I've never in my life met a woman like you."

"We're all the same."

"Do you think men are all the same?"

She considered and then looked up into his eyes. She said very seriously, "No."

Five

With the men so tired and needing sleep, Clint and Wallis settled themselves in the shed with the horses and Leo. Having had adequate sleep, they lounged on the bales of hay. There, they could talk.

Leo was pacing or sitting or standing as he looked around.

"Where did you get him," she asked Clint.

"It's the kind of story to tell on a day like today, but we really ought to be in front of the stove with a couple of beers."

"I can't stand beer."

He sighed with great drama. "God, but you've got a lot to learn. I just hope I have the staying power to make a dent in your ignorance."

She licked her lips and looked around, but he saw that her eyes danced with her responding humor. Her humor was encouraging to him.

He looked down her and said in his husky voice, "You ought to be illegal."

"I am."

"You're sure as hell the sassiest woman I've ever had to handle."

"You're not to 'handle' me. You're to keep your hands to yourself."

"You liked it when I rubbed your stomach."

"How rude of you to notice that." He had the kind of laugh that slid a lick around inside a woman's stomach and touched on shocking places, making them shiver erotically—with just a laugh? How could that be?

She smoothed her hands down her long-john-covered, clamped knees and pressed her canvas-clad feet close together.

He watched her and smiled with such tenderness that his weathered face was gentle. His blue eyes were probably tenderly benign for the first time in all his life.

She prompted, "Tell me about Leo."

"Don't you want my life story? We may never have a whole morning—with just talking—in all the rest of our time together."

"First Leo."

He sighed in disgust. "You could flirt just a little and say you're just dying to hear about me."

"I'm smarter than that."

"Damn."

She turned her head quickly to share his drollness. But almost instantly she was back to looking at her hands, which protected the barrier of her knees.

With her so careful not to look at him and flirt, he was free to keep his own gaze on her. And his eyes relished their good fortune. "You're as eye-catching as the buzz of a rattler."

"Why, sir, I do believe you've just given me a most charming compliment."

"And you're sassy."

She looked down and blushed just a bit with her pleasure over being the subject of his attention. She said again, "Tell me about Leo."

"My tongue can think of other things it'd rather do."

"Lick a Popsicle?"

"No. Something hotter."

Her blush went scarlet. "Tell me about Leo."

He sighed in resignation. "My cousin, Charlie, got him as a new pup. The dog was just from his mother and he attached himself to Charlie. Everywhere Charlie went, that little fat yella pup went along. It was funny to see such a butterball following a big, long man like Charlie.

"When the dog wasn't quite grown, Charlie got hisself killed in a car wreck out in the middle of nowhere. Somebody in a chopper finally spotted the car. It was a convertible. It was down a ravine. Charlie hadn't lived through the wreck. He never would wear a seat belt."

Completely still, Clint sat there on the hay bale and looked soberly out from under his hat at the wind-blown rain.

Wallis waited, not knowing if she should say something or not. It had to be some time since that wreck.

Finally, in a roughened voice, Clint told her, "You'll meet John Brown when we get to the big house. He's a fine man. A smart man who's financial adviser to my boss. His brother, Tom, is a photographer. Not long ago, Tom was out taking pictures of animal tracks when he found Leo. It'd been three years since the wreck.

"By then, we suppose, people had tried to trap the dog, and he was spooked by people. But Tom had the patience to allow the dog to get to know him.

"Tom discovered there was a puma in that area, and it really worried him that the dog would tangle with the cat. But he wouldn't snare the dog. He wanted the dog to come with him voluntarily.

"Then he and his girl, Susan Lee, were out leaving food for the dog when a big wild boar came roaring out of the brush, and the dog distracted the boar, giving Tom time to get to the car top. Tom says it was really hairy.

"Susan Lee was in the car with a rifle, firing bullet after bullet into the boar and not even slowing him down!" Clint shook his head once at the thought of it all.

Wallis said, "Was Tom hurt?"

"No, the postman came along in his car as the boar was chasing the dog across the road, and the postman hit the boar. They *still* had to shoot it in the brain, and even then they weren't certain it was really and truly dead. Boars are thataway."

"What an awful experience!"

"They took the boar back where Tom was staying and had a big pig roast. Leo went along with Tom."

"How'd you find out it was your cousin's dog?"

"When Tom came over to visit John, the dog came along and decided to stay with Lemon. Shows the kind of man Tom is, he allowed it. Lemon said it about killed Tom to let the dog go."

Clint gave a long sigh. "I'd just come back from a holiday. Tom had named the dog Hunter, and he came into the room and acted like he knew me. Then I remembered Leo.

"I called him Leo, and he barked once. I said Charlie's name and he barked again, just once. He'd remembered the names."

Clint sat there, idle, silent, looking out at the rain.

Wallis said, "You loved Charlie."

"God, yes. He was a great man. A friend. Support. A relative a man could count on. They don't come no better than Charlie."

She considered Clint. After some time, she said softly, "I'll bet he felt that same way about you."

"Don't get me emotional."

"There's nothing wrong with emotion."

He discarded her advice. "I can't handle it."

That was probably when she began to fall in love with Clint. Any man who could admit to emotion must have a good deal inside that iron hide of his. She was so sensitized to his emotion that she didn't notice the first wisps of fog.

He noticed. The wind was dying. The taggle end of the winds was the reason the fog was so subtle. He didn't mention fog to her. Not then.

While her concentration was on him, his attention was anywhere that would distract him from his dead cousin and the emotion that had risen with telling the story and remembering Charlie.

Leo turned and looked at Clint as if sharing the grief. How could that be? Clint had said Charlie's name. Did the dog still remember? Well, Clint did, why not Leo?

As if their thoughts were parallel, Wallis asked, "Are you all right?"

He turned and looked at her. And he really saw her. She wasn't just an attractive woman he'd found in trouble and saved, she was herself. His lips parted and he stared at her, scared. That embarrassed him. How could a little thing like her scare a man like him? Then he recalled, she'd asked if he was okay. He told her, "Not yet, but soon."

Now what did he mean by that? She looked out at the calming trees and tried to figure him out without getting into trouble by asking him for the answer. With men, sometimes it's better not to ask. A woman might find out more than she could handle.

Clint got up from the bale and walked around restlessly. He forked down more hay and ran his hands over the horses.

She was shocked when she realized she wanted him to do that to her. Surely not.

He got some burlap and began to rub down the horses, expending some of his pent-up frustration.

Wallis watched him as she brought up the sides of the blanket she was sitting on and wrapped herself in it.

He hadn't appeared to be watching, but he said, "I could do a better job of keepin' you warm."

"You're probably like that joke."

"I'm a joke?" He straightened and looked over the horse in such shock.

"The wham-bam-thank-you-ma'am type."

"No."

She knew he was waiting for her to ask what he was like. She didn't dare. She'd been rash enough. She said, "The rain's letting up. We might be able to get out of here tomorrow."

"We'll see if the river's down yet. From that gully washer, it's probably still flooded. We may be here a while, yet."

And she considered how dangerous that would be for her to be alone with him for even a day. Just this afternoon. The three sleeping men would wake at noon, eat and leave. None would come back because the other men had already begun moving the herd away during the night.

She would be left there alone with Clint. No one would come or interrupt his— Well, she was an adult and in control. He wouldn't— Not if she was firm, he would not. Control was the answer to almost anything.

She said, "I'm sorry Frankenstein will have to carry us both."

"We'll love it."

Wallis looked at Clint, but his upper face was covered by his hat, and his hands were busy rubbing down the horse.

The horse was very like a cat having his back scratched.

She went over to the edge of the shed and picked some mesquite leaves, drawing them along between her hand and thumb. She saw that it had stopped raining.

The winds had died. Everything was drenched and water was dripping off leaves and the shed roof, but it had stopped falling from the clouds.

The storm would be over. Soon, it would be finished. And she would have no excuse to stay around this restless man. He would have other things to do besides rescuing and entertaining and caring for her.

She felt a great, painful pang of regret at the thought of leaving Clint.

That shocked her. What on earth was the matter with her? Probably something in the coffee beans? The morning coffee could have removed varnish. It had been delicious. But anyone would instantly recognize, with the first sip, that she was doing a foolish thing to drink something that strong.

And Clint had had three cups. No wonder his voice had the sound of abused vocal chords.

As she walked back to the hay bale and sat down, he began to sing to the horses, and he had a wonderful voice for country songs. His singing could calm a horse or lure a woman. He sang, "Hush little baby, don't you cry—" and he added all sorts of rhyming words that were simply outrageous. She laughed silently, so that she didn't miss any of his wicked words.

He smiled just a tad and kept track of her amusement. He was so cocky and naughty, and his hands were gentle as they moved on to the next horse.

She considered all she knew of him, and she knew he was a special man. If he still grieved for his cousin, she wondered what kind of man Charlie could have been....

But she knew Charlie could never have matched Clint.

Charlie must have seemed as similar to Clint as any man could be, and that drew Clint's admiration. Clint needed someone close who could match him. Charlie probably almost made it.

Then Wallis examined her assumption. Was she prejudiced just because Clint had saved her neck and taken care of her?

No.

She was an impartial judge and could balance pros and cons with care and not become involved emotionally. This Clint was a man. How amazing to find such a man in this time.

That was the crux of it. He was a throwback to the times when men walked tall. When it wasn't just their good names and their computer genius they risked, but they took on responsibility and backed it with their bodies and their lives.

She decided she didn't want Clint to use his body or his life to solve anything. Well . . . not now.

That he'd ridden Frankenstein over that rough track while he'd risked facing that poor, distraught puma, in order to save Wallis Witherspoon's hide was okay. That one time. By him. But no one else.

Wrapped now in the blanket, she sang along with the songs she recognized as Clint sang to the horses.

She laughed and asked, "Do you always sing those songs to horses?"

"I'm singing to you."

And she went still. Her body was excited and her nerve ends quivered. She was probably cold. How odd to be cold when she wasn't chilling.

He began another song. It was an old one from years ago. The man wanted the woman. The song was how he saw her purple eyes and how he saw her body. It was a hot song, and his singing it that way as he rubbed down the third horse was very erotic.

How could a man grooming a horse make a woman hot? Clint could.

She was . . . hot?

Surely not. She took a deep, calming breath. And her breasts were pushy. Fortunately, she had the blanket around her. She was embarrassed by her body's hunger.

Why now? Why this rough man?

And she watched that rough man gently handling a horse while he sang to a woman. Her.

Men were underhanded and clever.

Clint sang to her and made her wish she were the horse, over there, and getting all that physical attention.

Wallis could have it.

She could.

All she needed to do was indicate that she was ready. That she was willing. That she wanted him.

She couldn't possibly be so bold.

Why not? She was twenty-nine years old. She'd never before wanted a man to do—it—to her. Not before now.

It was probably the thick coffee.

The coffee was the only thing she could think it could be. It wasn't the adventure of being rescued or riding on the back of his horse or wearing his jacket or—

It was probably the coffee.

Why couldn't he put that damned burlap bag down and come over to her with his calloused hands and rub her tender skin gently—at first.

Had there been locoweed in the coffee?

Of course not. That generally made people or cows tipsy and unable to control their steps.

She got up to test her ability to walk and found it was unimpaired. It wasn't locoweed. But it must be the coffee, because she was intensely aware of Clint and of the fact that he was male. And that she, in turn, was female.

It was a shock. She'd always considered herself as a woman who was human. Not as a woman who was sexually different from a man.

It was a little annoying that she'd waited until she was twenty-nine years old, for crying out loud, before she realized she could be sexually attracted.

She paced in a studied manner, listening to Clint singing a song that had a lot of hums, here and there, between words. Why was he humming half the time? Well, it could be because he'd forgotten the words. However, as she listened, she realized it was a really explicit song. Or it would be if he didn't hum so much.

What was he thinking? What could he be thinking while singing that wicked song? Probably exactly what was running around in her mind, only it was probably a little . . . a whole lot . . . earthier.

She was just distracted by sensations she'd never consciously recognized. Clint was probably witnessing the song's X-rated words in three-D with a salacious sound track. How shocking.

Wallis went over and sat back down on the bale of hay. There was once a mostly clothed film star who'd been rolled around in the hay some long years ago, and the entire male population had loved watching the film.

Maybe it wasn't the coffee. Maybe it was the hay!

But Wallis didn't get up. She sat there on that wild and woolly bale of hay, and her morals stood staunchly . . . wilting? Surely not. How incredible. Who ever heard of hay doing this to a woman?

It wasn't the hay that was luring her, it was the man over yonder mostly humming another slow song with probably concupiscent innuendo.

So it was in a horse shed that Wallis Witherspoon decided she would see if she could taste a roughly gentle man.

Over in Somalia, her mother would be so shocked.

She wouldn't think about her mother. . . .

It was only then that Wallis realized it was quite possible her mother had never liked sex. Well, how amazing to suddenly understand her mother. Wallis had never considered it before then. But she was suddenly sure that her mother had found sex very distasteful.

So Wallis wondered if her father had ever sung and hummed songs to her mother. Probably not. Was he clumsy? Uncommunicative?

Or had her mother been disinterested?

Well, their daughter would just see what this was all about. What if she was frigid? Her body was squirming inside itself and trying to communicate a very hot interest.

How was she going to signal Clint that she wanted to try him?

Was sex this complicated? Especially between such strangers. What should she do... first?

Well, she could hardly go over and ask, "Now?"

He'd probably fix her lunch.

She'd remembered a happening that had puzzled her at the time and had lain in her memory to surface occasionally. She'd been at a picnic. It was ten years ago. One woman had gotten up and walked out of the crowd. After a while, a man had followed her.

At that time, Wallis had been old enough to realize what was happening, but she hadn't seen any signal. Was the signal just the fact of the woman leaving? How had he known? Had the woman told the man before the gathering, "When I get up, you come after me!"

That seemed so crass. So calculated. So... unromantic. It was just... sex.

Well, look at Clint. He'd made it very clear that was what he wanted. He hadn't even kissed her, yet, but he'd talked about having sex with her. He was really very bold, and she found herself wondering if he did actually have condoms.

What a remarkable turnabout in her thinking. From a total rejection to plotting her own seduction. Maybe it was those three days in the hotbox car that had altered her genes?

What if, when it came down to the actual act, they found that she took after her mother?

She looked over at Clint, and her eyes ran down his body to his crotch. She felt a strange surge in the pit of her stomach. She probably wasn't a cold woman.

She might very well be the exact opposite and turn into a slaveringly voracious sex fiend.

She allowed her eyelids to lower as she looked at his body through her eyelashes. She wondered if he was hardy enough to satisfy all her fantasies.

She'd had fantasies? Well, she had! She remembered some of them. They were a surprise. She looked back at Clint and breathed.

He glanced up and caught her look. He smiled and licked his lips.

She licked her own in little, quick darts.

He straightened up and stared at her.

She looked quickly away and shifted abruptly, as if demonstrating how casual she was. Her breathing was erratic. She glanced quickly back at him. He was standing there, absolutely gorgeous, and he was watching her with a quizzical expression on his marvelous face.

She looked away, her eyes wide and staring casually at—whatever.

He dropped the burlap bag and came over to her like a male puma or a chancy dog. He sat down beside her, and she could hear him breathe and she smelled the maleness of him.

He asked, "You going to give me that kiss to thank me for saving your neck?"

Wallis looked at Clint starkly. He was being logical. They probably ought to kiss first. She swallowed noisily in a very casual way, and with her eyes about as open as they could get, she said, "Okay."

She looked at his mouth and his eyes, and his mouth and his eyes again, and she didn't move at all. She watched his mouth smile a little, and then she saw that his eyes were brimming with fire. Blue fire? She'd never in her life heard anything about blue fi—

And he kissed her.

His hands moved and his arms slid around her lax body. His mouth consumed her and those parts in her lower stomach that had fluttered and squirmed became intent and thrilled.

Her heart pounded out an erratic rhythm, and her breaths puffed from her nose, but her mouth clung to his.

He groaned and held her tighter.

She clawed closer to him and her breathing went awry. Her heart went into overdrive. Her hands clutched his shirt back, and her arms strained for him to get closer.

Closer?

How?

Well, where? There were three sleeping men in the shack. The shed had one whole side open. Where?

Clint said softly, "Umm. You're so sweet."

The first thing that caught her attention was that he could sort out words and then say them in sequence.

She pulled her head back to indicate she had to breathe or she'd faint. And he lifted his head back barely at all. Her eyes were like an owl's. She was ready.

He looked over at the shack and knew it was impossible to follow up on this amazing chance at the moment. How was he going to encourage her, survive the encouragement and stay alive until they could make love properly?

He said, "If you kiss me again, I'll explode."

"So'll I."

She shocked him. From her earlier talk, he'd thought she was a virgin. One he'd have to coax and comfort and handle with great care. She was a wild woman and she wanted it now!

Why?

That did puzzle him. She'd been so aloof and in control until this minute. Well, a minute ago. He needed to know what had set her off. He needed that information to do it again or never to risk it with another woman.

How was he supposed to ask her? *Well, look, what set you off this-a way? I'm taking a survey and the information is important to men. If somebody like you could get to this stage, men need to know what triggered you?*

There was no way he could ask. What he wanted to do was just go ahead and take advantage of the situation. He wanted to make love to her. Ever since he'd heard her voice calling from that dirty, old car, he'd been intrigued by her. Now he was hooked on wanting her.

He asked cautiously, "Do you know what you're doing to me when you rub against me thataway?"

She groaned. "What are you doing to me?"

He asked rather cautiously, "What?"

"I'm not sure, but I want you against me."

There is nothing in this world worse than an unknowing woman tempting a needy man. His hands began to shake and his breathing became irregular.

"Those guys are in the shack, and there isn't one place around here that I can make love with you. It's too wet outside for you. We don't have a truck around or any other place that you wouldn't get all muddy or wet."

"You don't want to." She began to loosen her arms.

"Wallis, my God, woman. Feel me."

So she put her hands on his . . . face. That was a very telling clue, right there.

He'd never been squashed against such a needy, unknowing woman in all his born days, and he probably couldn't survive this time at all well. He was going to be pulled through a knothole, and she'd probably be embarrassed and not recover from it. On top of all that, those guys in the shack most likely had their noses pressed against the window, facing the shed, watching like dogs with a hog being butchered.

His big rough-skinned hand smoothed her hair back from her pale face, and he said, "You're beautiful. You take my breath away."

In a voice that was gasping, she urged, "It isn't your breath I want."

"What do you want?"

How could he be that dumb? She was a little indignant, but being in that condition, she was sloppily so, and she said, "I want you."

"Tonight."

Her eyes popped open and she looked at him in shock.

He explained, "We have guests that would be jealous and envious, and they could well try to share."

"Share . . . what?"

"You."

"You wouldn't let them."

"I'd try."

She urged, "Kiss me."

"I think you've had enough."

She was indignant. "You don't . . . want me."

"Oh, yes." He was sure.

But he didn't know her family, and she began to withdraw from him even before she physically started to pull back from him.

He said, "I want you very badly. I watched you laying in the water, and I wanted you then."

"Then? I was all sweaty and disgusting."

"No. You were brave and noble and beautiful."

"With my hair all wet and me shivering."

"Against my back and pushing against me. Your body was so soft. I thought I couldn't force you then, that I might have to wait for you to decide if you wanted me."

"You actually, really and truly wanted me then, when I was so grungy?"

"You were exciting to me."

"I don't believe you. You're just trying to make your rejection easier for me. Thank you. I'll leave you alone."

"Only for a while." She sat away from him, and he saw that she was blushing painfully. He'd embarrassed her with his delay.

"If I made love to you here, the guys might see us. Think about that. They'd expect you to be friendly with them. Wallis, I'm trying to protect you."

"Do you have condoms with you?"

"In my saddlebag."

"Let me have a couple. I'll see if one of those others will have me."

She didn't mean it at all. She was pushing him. He understood. He was going to have to work to get her attention again and coax her again to passion.

She distanced herself more, then she rose from the bale and pulled the blanket around her.

She considered that she was being entirely unreasonable, but she went on being that way.

He watched as she went to the center post on the open side of the shed and she leaned against it.

Beyond her, one of the men was standing outside the shack, and he was watching Wallis.

Six

Clint knew positively that the ranch hand had not been out of the shack when he'd first kissed Wallis. But somehow, after that kiss, Clint had lost track for a while.

With them in the back of the shed, the man couldn't have seen them clearly enough. The sky was heavily overcast, the shadows in the shed were dark. The walls had only narrow windows for people to see out.

Even with the full side opening, they'd been against the hay. He couldn't have known they were kissing. Unless it was that eagle-eyed Trevor out there, under that hat.

Clint rose from the bale of hay and stretched his hard body, showing it off in a threatening way for the watcher to note. He walked lazily over and stood behind Wallis in the stronger if dimmed daylight. He didn't touch her, for fear she'd jerk away from him and that yahoo would come a-running to her rescue.

It was Trevor out there, still watching deliberately.

Clint shifted and he moved his mouth as he pretended he was saying soft words to that stubborn, turned-away woman. Then Clint walked slouchingly out of the shed and stretched again before he stopped in the middle of it as if he'd just caught sight of Trevor.

He grinned like the dog he was and strolled over toward Trevor, asking in a softly carrying voice, "You get enough sleep or aren't you used to a mattress?"

Trevor's stare came to Clint. He said a nothing, "Yeah." But he looked on past Clint, back to the woman.

Oh, hell. Trevor was an itchy man. Clint moved his feet as if the two were having an amicable conversation. In a low voice, he told Trevor, "Watch yourself."

How could such soft words carry such a threat?

Trevor asked, "That dog dangerous?" He meant that Clint was not.

Clint noted only then that Leo was between Wallis and Trevor, and he was watching Trevor. He was protecting Wallis? Yeah. It was logical, since Leo had been the primary reason she'd been rescued. But the dog had allowed Clint to kiss her.

To Trevor's question, Clint replied, "He's dangerous on occasion."

"Then you ought to shoot him."

Clint shook his head. "He's dangerous to rattlesnakes, rats and other...vermin."

That was warning enough. The woman had a man and a dog to protect her. It was a toss up which of the two was more lethal.

"How'd she get here?"

"Leo found her in a stuck car that was by a puma's den. He got me to help him save her. Lemon can tell you about it."

Trevor finally turned his head and looked into Clint's flinty eyes. His smile was thin, but he asked, "How grateful is she?"

Clint allowed the mouthiness. He replied, "She let the dog sleep with her, and she said, 'Thank you' to me."

Then Trevor's smile widened, and he couldn't help the real humor that intruded.

Clint smiled, too, and he knew the exchange would be repeated at all the campsites, and probably expanded on. But Clint didn't mind. Last night's crew would confirm that Leo had slept with her.

Trevor went into the shed, touching his hat to the sober-faced woman who only nodded one dip in reply. He went to his horse and exclaimed, "Who rubbed him down?"

Clint said, "I needed to get rid of some extra energy?" That was a do-you-understand, questioning statement.

And Trevor slapped Clint's shoulder as he laughed in derisive hoots.

That, too, would be added to the chatter by the campsites. Old Clint was flustered. And by a woman! Imagine that. Clint!

The other men came out in a dribble, complaining about not being able to sleep on those soft mattresses. They could hardly wait to get back to sleeping on the cold, hard ground. It was stifling in that there huge, closed-up building. They were glad to be outside so they could finally breathe again. And they stood around, doing that.

One of the older men chided Wallis, "You shouldn't've come over and snuck into my bed thataway. I'm plumb wore out."

She gasped and sputtered in indignation so that the other men hooted and loved it.

Clint limited himself to one word, "Careful." And that was warning enough. But he was lazy as he said it and his eyes were amused. However, since it was from Clint, the word put the kabosh on anything more that was rowdy.

The men were pleased their animals had been so cared for. They'd wiped them down early that morning, but they'd been too tired to do such a good job. They took the saddle blankets off the inside shed lines and took them out to shake them. Then they resaddled and tidied their equipment.

They'd slept hard and eaten hot food, and their horses were rested. They mounted and were cheerful as they waved and rode away.

And they left behind a man, a dog and a young woman...alone.

Clint said, "How about lunch? Would you like a hamburger, or soup and cheese, or stew?"

"Is this some sort of test? I believe I'll get chili, and it will be called whatever I select. You'll be enormously surprised when I question why the meal was called 'hamburger' instead of chili."

"How can you be that smart, when I know you're still exhausted from your long vigil?"

"Vigil." She considered the word. "Do you really speak the way the men do, or do you mix the words in order to fool me?"

"I throw in words so as you'll think I know as much as you."

That was as honest as a man could get. It was true.

Of course, she didn't believe him. She thought he played with words instead of having to screen them frantically so that his speech wouldn't shock her.

He didn't want to shock her. Then he wondered if he would be that careful after she'd allowed him to sleep with her? Make love with her? Use her? Would it ever come to a time that he could just...use her...and leave?

The very idea of leaving her scared his chest.

Then he was distracted as he slitted his eyes and tried to think what had ever, before then, scared him?

Whatever it had been, he'd forgotten it. He did notice the men had cleaned up after themselves and, by that time, he'd made the tortillas, and she'd heated up what was left of the rice, bean and chili dish. Then she had to cook more rice and beans because what was made was entirely too pepper hot to suit her tongue.

She was a little distant with Clint. He was gentle, sweet and kind. All men do that when they're trying for a woman. Wallis knew it.

He made a list of supplies for the crew to replenish when they picked up the used bedding. He hung the blankets in the shed to air. And he talked to John Brown on the satellite phone.

Clint bragged on the crew men and their conduct. He reported on the things about the herd that were relevant. And he gave a list of supplies for that cabin.

John asked, "How's our guest?"

Clint replied, "Tired. Being trapped in the car was wearing for her. The hands were kind to her and their eyes popped to see her. She's something."

"You know the crossing is still flooded and you ought not try it. It's bad enough, but the fog would make it impossible. If she needs to make any contact, we can call them for her."

"I'll ask." Clint was patient.

"She is okay?"

"Just tired. She's asleep in the shack. I'm out in the shed." That made it sound as if she had the house while he stayed in the shed.

"Did she sleep in the house when the crew was there? Were they in the house with her? That's a rowdy bunch."

"Leo slept with her."

John laughed. Then he said, "How bad is the fog out there? We're at a dead standstill."

"Just wisps."

"Don't try to cross the river. You'd see the fog before then, but you could go into the river before knowing it was there. The water is still running high."

"We'll have to stay here?"

John comforted him. "You sleep in the shed."

"Yeah." Clint's heart fluttered and his body withstood slithering excitements.

Wallis napped while Clint rode Frankenstein to give him some exercise as he looked around the area, but he left Leo to guard their guest.

From a distance, he gauged the fog. It was really thick and moving out from the river. Thoughtfully, Clint rode back to the shack.

Wallis was up, outside and hanging clothes on the line.

He smiled at her and asked, "Good nap?" He didn't mention the fog.

She gave him a dismissive glance with her chin tilted up and she said, "I missed . . . Leo."

The dog hadn't been in her bed but outside! She was taunting him? He said, "Get your gear together. We'll try the river down a ways." She needed to realize how completely trapped she was there, with him.

"You've been down to the river?"

"No. That was too far. I stayed close enough to hear Leo."

"I wonder if the river's gone down?"

"We'll see." He had a compass for fog. They wouldn't get lost.

"Where will you take me?"

"To Covington's. They have a lot of room, and they're good people. We'll find out if your car stayed put or where it went. And we'll salvage it if it can be fixed."

He'd already told her it would never have lasted through that gully washer. Was he now trying to keep her from knowing she was stranded?

She went inside while he fiddled around not doing much. When she emerged from the shack, she was again dressed in her clean, unpressed slacks and shirt. She wore the tennies.

He asked, "Do you need to notify anyone? Is anyone worrying about you?"

"Not right away."

"I can contact Lemon's place, and they can leave any message anywhere at all."

"In another day."

"That long? You're a little careless, aren't you?"

"Not until recently."

Did she mean she'd been careless in getting her car stuck or did she mean it was careless for her to be there with him? "You can't help it that Leo had to save your neck."

"He had help."

Clint smiled in his mind. He said, "I'm honored to be included."

And she laughed.

He reached to help her get on the horse. She said, "Shouldn't we put out the fire in the stove?"

Oops. He said, "I thought the guys did that. I should have checked. It would be a sin if the shack burned down." He looked at her to share the smile.

But she was looking at the shack. And very softly, she said, "Yes."

The urgent shivers hit his body. Because she'd like a *shack?* Now that was silly.

So he went inside, and they finished tidying up as if they would actually be leaving. He had to do that to allow her to realize she was stuck with him. From a stuck car in a riverbed to being stuck in an isolated shack with a prairie wolf. She had no luck at all.

He smiled. "I suppose you're looking forward to a soaking bath in bubbles?"

"I'm a shower woman."

"So you like rain?"

"Actually, yes."

It was too bad to ruin the fire. They'd just have to come back and rebuild it. He took the smoking logs outside in the bucket and doused them with water from the rain barrel.

He looked around. Everything was tidy. He helped her up on the horse. Under her own clothing, she had on a pair of long johns. Over her own pants and shirt, she was wearing his jacket against the chill, and his bandanna was around her head. She wore his gloves.

Since he'd gotten the kinks out of Frankenstein, he could walk the horse along. It wasn't far before the fog was noticeable. It was in fragments, still, but it was moving slowly away from the river.

She questioned, "Fog?"

And in perfect honesty, he replied, "Yeah."

"It's thicker on beyond."

"Yeah."

"We could get lost."

"Yeah. Maybe we should go back."

They were in the outer edges of it. He could feel her looking around. "Do you know which way?"

"I think so." He stretched up and really looked around, but he consulted the compass in his hand.

Very cleverly, he moved Frankenstein in various directions. He'd say, "Nope. That's too different." But he kept close track, and they "stumbled on" the shack.

She was astonished they'd found it again. She was glad to be there.

But even as they dismounted, they could see the air thickening. She said, wide-eyed, "It's lucky we came back."

And he looked around before he agreed, "Yeah."

They took Frankenstein into the shed. He'd had adequate exercise. He was unsaddled and wiped down. Then Clint stretched the rope barrier across the open side to indicate to Frankenstein that he was to stay put. He would. But that way, he had the freedom of the shed and could look out any of the slots.

Leo was content to stay in the shed.

The two humans went back to the shack. Clint helped Wallis from his jacket and hung it on one peg while he put his Stetson on another. She handed him his kerchief, and he put it on top of his hat. The fog had dampened their exposed clothing.

She was thoughtfully silent.

As he rebuilt the fire in the stove with dry wood, he could not resist multiple glancings over at her. He smiled inside and licked his lips like an anticipating cat.

She said soberly, "I'm sorry you're stuck here with me."

That did startle him, and he opened his mouth to soothe her.

But she said, "You must have so much to do."

"If that fog's spread over the whole place, nobody is doing nothing but trying to keep track of things."

"You were brilliant to get us back to the shack. Look outside."

Although he knew exactly what it looked like, he closed the stove and went to the window. It was perfect. The fog now crowded the window.

The only fly in the ointment was whether the last crew was far enough away that they wouldn't try to get back.

None of them needed to come back, but who could resist the lure of sitting around just watching how Wallis moved and listening to her speak. She was so different from the usual allotment of men.

The crew could find their way back to the herd. He'd followed cattle in fog. A man just watched to cut across their trail. Beeves tended to leave a wide sign that they'd been along thataway. Then you could get off your horse and inspect the hoofprints to see which direction they were going. You could do that in the night by feeling the prints. You could do the same in a fog. Whether the herd was lost or not wouldn't matter. You would eventually find them and could keep track of them. Then, too, there would be other men around them to share that fun.

Clint lighted the kerosene lamp. It was very silent. The fog really was a sound-covering blanket. Clint knew there was a radio on the top of the cabinet, but he didn't want her distracted from him.

If things got really dull, he could "find" the radio.

He pulled a chair around by the stove and with his back to the lamp and shaking out a newspaper, he inquired, "Are you trembling with excitement to hear the news from . . . last February?"

"Sounds fascinating."

He shifted pages. "This is local, so you can put it down to research. Bill Rodriguez lost a bull. Somehow it had lifted the latch on his pen and gotten away." He shook the paper and looked for another item as he explained about Bill. "That means the bull was stolen and everybody realized it and will look for it, but the thieves think they're home free."

After a slight pause that was filled with silence, Wallis commented, "If I was a thief, I'd suspect they were printing it for that very reason."

He bragged on her, "See? You're too smart to steal a good bull."

"I wonder if they caught the thieves?"

With some droll humor, he responded, "If we're fogged in here long enough, we just might find out."

And she laughed.

He lowered his paper to smile at her, and something happened low in her stomach that was very like what had happened out in the shed just that morning. Surely not. She could control herself. "When I left the car, I should have brought my knitting."

"You knit?"

"Brilliantly. I also crochet, needlepoint and tat!"

"What's tat?"

"Tatting," she corrected gently. "It's making lace with all sorts of simple knots."

He was blank.

"One uses a shuttle. It's quite small. Sailors use shuttles that are enormous and weave ropes into knots for sails."

"I remember doing that."

"You . . . sailed?"

"It was a choice I was given once."

"What was the other one?"

"Jail."

"Wow! What all had you done?"

"I'd beaten the tar out of a very important man's really nasty bas—son."

"So they sent you off."

"If they hadn't, I might have killed him."

"What had he done?"

Clint looked over at her. His face was deadly serious. "It isn't for your ears. Just know he deserved . . . more."

"Where is he now?"

"He died in a traffic pileup that he caused. He was stinking drunk and probably didn't feel a thing. I'm glad."

"You've forgiven him?"

"No. I'm glad he died. I wish it had been in slow motion for him. I wish he'd suffered like—I wish it had been as bad as it could have been. Or maybe that he would have lived in pain."

She looked at him. "What on earth had he done to you?"

"Nothing. Not to me. If we know each other for a long time, maybe I'll tell you—some of it."

"I'm sorry you went through something that bad."

"It wasn't to me."

"But you suffered for someone else."

He was abrupt. "No."

"It made you angry enough to have to go to sea. To be sent away."

"I enjoyed the sea."

"Why did you come ashore?"

He replied,. "I wanted control."

"I can understand that. May I sketch you?"

"If I don't have to pose."

"I thought I might make you into a tiger lily."

"Uh. Let's cancel doing it."

"You are uncomfortable being a tiger lily?"

He considered her as his smile began. "No. Go ahead." And his eyes sparkled with interest.

She looked at him thoughtfully. "You're hoping I show this in an exhibit, and you'll stand by it, just waiting to see if anyone comments. Then you'll rearrange their teeth?"

"That just about covers it."

She sighed in defeat. "I'll see if Leo would like to be a sunflower."

"I'd prefer he stay in the shed with Frankenstein. In this fog, anything or anyone could show up. I don't want the horse, or us, to be surprised."

"There's danger?"

"Out in the sticks, thisaway, there's always danger."

She looked around seriously. She suggested, "Should we turn off the lamp?"

"Not with a horse and dog in the shed. They're a dead giveaway. That and the smoke coming from the chimney."

"Yes."

His voice gentle, he told her, "Don't be nervous. You're safe here with me."

"Don't all lechers say something like that?"

"How would I know?"

And again, she laughed.

He watched her. She was a jewel. She could laugh after hearing he'd had the choice between jail and the sea, after he'd beaten someone. She had accepted his word that this thrashing of another human had been right. She trusted him.

Trust. Now that was an ugly thing to think about, when he was bound and determined to get her, right over there on that bunk bed. Was her trust going to make him postpone her taking? Damn.

Maybe she'd demand that he have sex with her. Yeah. She could do that, and he could give in by being graciously accommodating.

She didn't look like the type who'd demand anything. She might whine and plead? She wasn't a whiner, either. When she'd been trapped by the puma, she'd considered only the poor puma.

Maybe he could convince her he was dying of overload! It would be worth the try. He could—

She suggested, "If you're that far back on the news, why don't I reply to any questions you might have about the current events? I've only been out of touch with the world for seven days, counting the one I gathered samples before I got stuck."

So he asked, "Why did you take that old car down into the riverbed?"

"It seemed like a good idea at the time."

He was stern. "You ought not be running around the countryside alone. It was stupid."

"I could have had someone trapped inside with me when you came to the rescue, and how would you have handled two people?"

"I'd have figured out something."

And she knew he would have. So she told him, "Yes, you would have. You're a fine man."

She was going great until that last sentence. Now Clint had the burden of conscience on his head. If it wasn't one thing, it was another.

With any other woman he'd known, they'd already be napping after the third or fourth leisurely time. Sated. Contented. Depleted.

She stirred him so much, his eyeballs were probably bulging. How long had he been with her now? Well, alone, only a few hours.

That was time enough.

He said very seriously, "I need another kiss."

She turned her head and looked at him as if he'd grown another head.

He reached his hands up to confirm that he still had only one between his shoulders.

Her lips parted and she frowned just the slightest.

He explained, "You were looking at me like I had two heads."

"You sounded that way."

"An echo?"

"No. The good head and the bad head."

He laughed immoderately.

They played cards.

Now, Clint was a good card player. He was crafty, he had a brilliant memory, and he'd played cards seriously and for money since he was twelve. She won. How did she do it? He had no idea. She wasn't cheating. He watched her.

She was brilliant. She was amazing. She was a better player than he, and it irritated him.

But he lay back in his chair, appearing indifferent and flipped the cards on the table as if they didn't matter.

But he was playing on the razor's edge, and he sure as hell ought to be winning. But he was not.

Wallis began to mention little plays he could have made. She was being kind. That irked the bloody hell out of Clint.

He said, "I could whittle you a crochet stick."

She corrected, "Hook."

"Yeah." He slid in a card, but she saw it and that was that. He'd lost again. He said, "What size thread do you have?"

"Just that twine in the shed."

"Now what made you notice the twine?"

"I don't know. I always notice textures and color blendings and shadows."

"You're a real artist."

"A graduate from the school of fine arts."

"You said you were a horticulturist."

"A second degree."

And there Clint Terrell was, a third-grade dropout? He gave up on her. He couldn't bring himself to make love with her. She outdistanced him so far that he couldn't even touch a foot*print* of her shoe.

He said, "I'll fix supper."

"More rice and chili?"

"No. There's a canned ham, sweet potatoes and green beans. Can you make biscuits?"

"If they come in a roll that you twist."

"I can make biscuits."

"You would make some woman a wonderful husband."

He choked. While he'd choked at the idea of being married, it had been from a quickly indrawn breath of surprise, but he turned it into a real hambone shock.

She laughed at him until she almost couldn't whack his back and hold up his left arm to help him. With his arm up and her whacking, she jiggled. Her jiggling made him prolong the attack.

He liked her attention.

They made supper. Her biscuits were interesting. He had directed her, and she'd attacked the combination of flour, canned milk and powdered egg.

He baked them on the stovetop, using a rounded iron cover. It was an interesting experiment, and it worked. They'd forgotten the salt. They studiously added some to the jam and it was another venture. The rest of their meal was very good.

The horse got some grain, and the dog a can of food from Clint's saddlebag.

She inquired, "Do you keep the condoms in with the dog food?"

The thrill that concentrated in him was awesome. His voice was husky as he assured her, "No."

"Well, show me where they are, in case I have a surprise opportunity to use one and need one right away."

He wobbled.

Seven

Clint's tongue stumbled all over the verbal choices as he tried to tell Wallis exactly where the condoms were. Incapable of explaining, he showed her. Then he offered to give her several.

"Why do you carry condoms along in your saddlebag?" It seemed a logical question to Wallis.

He went blank. He said, "Uhh." He said, "Well, you see." He said, "It's like this."

"Where would you expect to find a willing woman?" Wallis was interested in his reply.

He thought about it and questioned carefully, "In a stuck car?"

And she laughed, yet again. She thought he was humorous. She said, "I've never met a man with such a clever tongue. You have an answer for everything."

No. He didn't. He was floundering all along the way. He didn't know how to impress her. He worried about that when he'd already done it by rescuing her from her car. He didn't need to keep on being clever. But he felt the need to shine in her eyes.

If he was any brighter, she wouldn't be able to see.

He gave her the three condoms as if parting with friends. Since they couldn't be used but once, that rather amused her. "Have you carried them for some time, that you're so attached to them?"

He couldn't think of a public reply to that one.

She said, "I'll replace them, if these are used."

He couldn't think of any comment on that, either. Plead that he be the subject of her adventure? He was the only one around, if she wanted to experiment. Thank goodness. And he remembered Mae West, that old doll, saying "goodness" had nothing to do with it.

Gradually, as they talked, Wallis became aware of his hesitancy. She asked, "Do you choose your words? You take a while to reply."

"Among ourselves, we use such rough words that I forget about it and sometimes I shock ladies."

The new woman of the world who possessed three condoms replied, "You couldn't shock me."

He was caught by her declaration, but he didn't reply as he would have to a man saying the same thing. Women have no idea how men talk together. Well, some of them might, but Clint didn't know any man who spoke the same way to women as he did to men.

While she said she was unshockable, he didn't want to risk offending her. Not when she was carrying three unused condoms around. He wanted to seem attractive to her. He didn't want her to think he was vulgar, crude or crass. Think of all the words that defined the way he spoke. He'd learned those, too.

She confided in an open manner, "Even I have said 'crap.'" And her smile was to make him feel comfortable with her.

She thought "crap" was vulgar! Hell, that was one of the nicer words.

She said, "Sing me some of your songs."

He bit into his lower lip and then he recalled all the humming he'd had to do to clean up those he'd sung to her in the shed. She wanted a song.

He rattled his brain and sang a version of "Bury Me Not on the Lone Prairie." He had to hum through some of that one, too. It was about a guy who wasn't dead enough to be buried. And the cattle were late getting to the feeder railroad. They'd already dug him his grave, but he hadn't yet been ready. It was a little like the poem, "The Cremation of Sam McGee."

She was entertained.

With the fog so close and reflecting, the night was strange. They went out to see about the animals, and they looked at the density of the fog. He found that fog very nice and enclosing. They could be there three or four days.

She said, "I'm glad the Comanches are friendly."

"This fog spook you?"

"Somewhat. I prefer to see beyond."

"Beyond . . . what?"

"My nose," she replied. "This is like being in white darkness."

"Yeah. That describes it. You ought to see fog on the sea. The waves seem to come out of nowhere. The fog is still and the water moves. When both are still, you think you're lost in another world . . . and alone."

His words surprised her. He could be lonely? This self-sufficient, able man could need another person?

Well, it was obvious that he needed female companionship... if female companionship was the expression to be used. He wanted women. And the word would be plural. Could he be faithful to one woman? Being faithful would be very out of character for him. Would it? She wondered.

He opened the door and looked inside carefully before he allowed her to go into the room. They'd been away, and the fog had concealed the shed. He made sure nothing had slipped inside. And he locked the door.

He was careful.

He found the radio. He found it in great surprise and turned to a music station. It was western stomp. He showed her the TEXAS two-step, and they danced it side by side.

She knew how to do the two-step and appeared to learn his version quite fast. He was impressed.

But with a slow dance, he took her into his arms and held her, moving his feet slowly and moving his hands with groans.

She leaned back to ask, "What's the matter?"

His eyes were serious in the feeble lamplight. He said, "I really badly need a kiss."

She smiled.

So he kissed her. He was steel muscled with his control. At first, he barely touched his body to hers, but he groaned in agony and pulled her closer. The tips of his fingers reached around under her arms and probed the sides of her squashed breasts.

She made some relishing sounds that about sundered him. But she wiggled to get closer, and his head almost blew.

He said, "Honey—" He said, "Listen, darlin—" He said, "I—" He said, "I don't think—" He said, "Could you—" He swallowed noisily and groaned.

She started unbuttoning his shirt!

His breaths hyperventilated him and he got a little dizzy.

She became concerned for him. She'd just assumed a man his age would be...well...experienced. Maybe he was all mouth? A'way out there in the sticks, there just weren't enough available women? And tramp steamers weren't military boats. Maybe there hadn't been any women on those boats.

She asked gently, "Is this your first time?"

So he said, "Be gentle."

"It's mine, too. We'll learn together."

She led a stunned man stumbling along over the familiar tracks as if it *was* all new to him. She encouraged his investigation of her body. She helped him take off the rest of his clothes; then she encouraged him to help her remove her own.

He almost didn't make it. He did roll on the condom. She was interested and very willing to assist him, but he was selfish. She told him that, and he promised she could do it the next time.

She asked in delight, "How often can we do it?"

And he warned, "Don't terrify me."

She led him to the bunk and lay down as if in her coffin, legs straight and arms by her side.

He melted. He admired her. He touched her and smoothed his hand along her, and he kissed more than her mouth. She wasn't sure he should do that and questioned him.

So he showed her how nice it was, and encouraged her mouth on him. She wasn't sure *at all* that she should, but he was patient and logical. So she did. And she was round eyed and excited by his response.

He made hoarse sounds and put his head back and groaned, and he kissed her differently, deeper, wetter.

She got restless and didn't know what to do next.

He showed her how to accept him, and she did. But she was so amazed and distracted that he rode the passionate wild winds all by himself.

When his hoarse panting had slowed and he could speak, he said, "Ah, honey, I'm just so sorry."

"Why?"

"That I didn't take you with me."

"Take?"

"That you didn't climax."

"It was really exciting."

"It can get better. Here, let me."

He massaged her gently, and she gasped at the sensation. She blushed vividly under his tender eyes, but she said, "Don't."

"It'll feel good."

"I'd rather... wait."

And his voice got foggy. "Wait?"

"'Til the next time."

He hugged her and groaned. She was like no other woman he'd ever known. He could fall in love with her. That was something he'd avoided ever since—

She chatted. "I'm glad this happened before I was thirty. It has worried me, being a '90s woman and still a virgin."

"I can't figure how a hot woman like you escaped."

"I believe it was getting stuck in the car. To face dying, one way or the other, and not to have experienced—this—would have been a regret."

"Think of all the young eighteen-year-olds who were sent into combat in wars who'd never known a woman. My granddaddy told me about that when I was eleven. He was dying."

"That was an odd thing for a grandfather to tell a child when he was on his deathbed. It would seem to me that he would have given you other information about schooling or jobs or patriotism or how to solve the national debt."

"He'd caught me with a neighbor's girl. His lecture was in not getting a strange female pregnant."

"So you carry condoms in your saddlebags."

"Most of the guys do that. With all the diseases around now, that's more of a worry than just getting a strange woman pregnant."

"So you think I'm riddled with disease."

"I'd risk it with you. But I wouldn't want you to get pregnant without you agreeing."

"Have you any—brush—children?"

"I've been very careful . . . most of the time," he tacked that on. "But when I was sudden, I waited to find out if she did get caught."

"And no one did?"

"Not yet."

"That sounds as if you just might take—another chance."

"Well, the fog is thick, and we're caught here and you got only three condoms."

She blushed and wiggled just a little. "When's the time to finish off the second condom?"

He lay back on his limited space and held on to the top of the bunk so that he didn't go off onto the floor. "Mother never told me about women like you."

"What did she tell you?"

"Quit that—stop that—leave him alone—pick that up—"

"She sounds harried."

"Tired?"

"Overburdened. Too much to take care of in limited time."

"Yeah. I'd never thought of her thataway."

She shifted to give him more room and pulled his head onto the center of her pillow. Her soft hand smoothed his face. She carefully finger combed his hair back from his white forehead and ran her feeling fingers over his sun-browned chin. Gently she inquired, "What happened to her?"

"I don't know."

"Did no one know, or didn't you ask?"

"I guess I lost interest when she shifted me to my granpaw."

"Didn't she take you back, after he died?"

Clint was getting restless with her questions. He replied shortly, "She'd taken off."

"You must have had siblings?"

He replied with slowed abruptness, "Brothers. I was oldest." Then, surprisingly, he went on. "One died riding a freight out of here when he was ten. I heard one died in Vietnam. One died caught in the chain of a well driller. One died in a car wreck. And one died shot by a husband. He was probably my full brother."

"The rest weren't?"

He considered how much he could shock her. Then he was a little abrupt. "My momma was . . . itchy. She was only married once. One thing, none of us died in jail."

What an interesting brag. Her fingers slowly played in his hair, her face was tender. "You've mentioned your boss as . . . Lemon? Is he a sour man?"

Clint stretched and was very like a big cat having his head rubbed. "No way. He's younger than me, and he has more money than he can count." But then his ego nudged him into telling her, "I'm his right-hand man. I can handle anything, and he respects me."

The last sentence was the ringer. It showed how important it was to Clint. "I'd like to meet . . . Lemon."

And Clint's eyes came to her as he said firmly, "He's got a woman and might not notice you."

"I didn't say I wanted to sleep with him. I just said I'd like to meet him."

"You will. He's curious about you. He's interested in weeds."

"Weeds?"

Slowly, thinking it out, he told her, "They call them the old grasses. Lemon's planting them. He's trying to bring them back. The old grasses are what fed the buffs and the longhorns. The grasses are strong and don't need the care of the hay we grow. The people've been hunting them in out-of-the-way places. One man found some growing wild down the center of a two rut road. They're the native grasses that covered this land before white man came and spoiled it all."

"Are you part Indian?"

Choosing his words, he replied carefully, "Naw. I'm a white man, but I love this land. My people've been here for a couple hundred years. Lemon says I'm a throwback to another time. I'd like to see the land wild and free. I'd like people to be that way, too. And I like beeves. I like them on the hoof and on my plate, juicy and seared."

"Seared. Raw?"

"Pretty near."

"I like cooked food."

"You're a spoiled woman."

She lowered her eyelids in a flirting manner. "I'm still waiting for that."

In a reedy voice, he asked, "Why don't you encourage me?"

"Smile and flirt?"

"That's a starter. But first I've got to clean up a little. Don't move."

He left her on the bunk and went to the stove. He opened it, put the used condom into the low flames and added some more wood.

He went to the sink and washed his hands and brought her a drink of water. Then he went back for a towel and dipped it into the water pan on the stove. It was hot. He opened the towel and waved it as he came to her and wiped her face and body.

Then he wiped his own. He did that so she could watch. Fascinating.

He was so...different. So male. So...well...he was a throwback. She remembered Clint had said Lemon's house was enormous. That he was wealthy and held large parties and weekend parties. The house was big enough to hold all that. And here was a rough man from another time. How interesting it would be to see him in another setting.

He smiled at her and his eyes glinted. "I like you watching me."

"You're beautiful."

He puffed disbelieving air from between his lips in rejection of such a label. "I'm manly. My grandfather told me that."

"When you were twelve?"

"By then, I was already six feet tall."

"How tall are you now?"

"Over six-three. How tall are you?"

"I'm five-seven."

He said, "Big enough." But then he teased gently, "Shorty."

She already knew he was a loner. Now she knew that his opinion of himself was as a survivor. He'd been tested—in his opinion—and not found wanting. He could handle anything. He'd allowed her to understand that. Now he teased that she was little and helpless, and he'd be in charge of her.

He thought that of a woman who'd traveled alone in a vast, sparsely peopled land and wasn't hysterical after three days trapped in a stuck car.

She would have to be tactful in allowing him to know that she didn't actually need him or his care. She could take care of herself. She was equal.

Moving his body with lax display, he came back and stood beside the bunk. He looked along her naked body, allowing her to see him. She was already taking advantage of the opportunity. With him close, she reached out and touched him.

He grinned at her and his eyes actually shot sparks of blue flame. She'd read about that happening and thought it was just the writer's wild imagination.

His hands were so big that one covered her stomach. Her shoulder fit into his palm, her breast was cupped and kneaded and gently squeezed.

It was his surprising gentleness that caught her. She'd heard tales of rough men. Clumsy men. She shouldn't have been surprised he handled her so well. She'd seen him with the horse and with Leo.

Not that she was a horse or a dog, but she was impressed that he could be so tender. And he took such pleasure in touching and feeling around on her. He looked at her and watched her body as his hands moved on her.

While she blushed scarlet, she was thrilled by him. And he touched her heart with his obvious interest.

He was a lover.

He leaned and kissed her body. She breathed brokenly and gasped and wiggled closer and she was shocking, to herself. He loved her reactions.

She whispered, "Are you supposed to do that?"

He lifted his mouth and said, "Yes. You can do it to me."

That made her shiver differently than one did with a chill. Her breaths, then, were in just the tops of her lungs in a rather panicky manner...or was it excitement? Surely not. Her fingers curled into the hard mattress and she became restless as she waited her turn.

And when she managed to get him flat so that she curled over him, he asked, "Where'd you learn to do that?" And he gasped, "I have proof you were a virgin. How'd you...know...to...do...that?"

Busily, she managed to reply, "You did it to me."

He loved it. He was elaborately shocked. "I never! I did *that* to you?"

"The female counterpart."

The actual word counterpart wasn't one he remembered ever hearing, but the word counter was familiar and he could guess what she meant. He said, "I'd never be that bold."

And she burst into laughter.

He found it was fun to tease a woman. He'd never before taken the time. He changed their encounter into a romp, and they played at love. It was different from anything he'd ever shared, and he began to fall in love with her, to seriously feel the binding strands of love.

She had had no release, so her pitch was one that he had to manage in order to play enough for his pleasure and still keep her in hand enough to delay her passion's release.

Her body was treasured and teased, and he encouraged her freedom with his own. She did explore. He had to leave the bed and invite her along because he had to use the privy. It was telling that he locked the cabin door and carried the key with him.

He coaxed her to go inside, but she declined. Wrapped in a blanket, barefooted, she waited outside, looking at the intense fog. It lightened the depth of the night, but closed in closely on her.

When they got back in the shack, unlocked and re-locked the door, she was predictably chilled while he was not. He told her she was a softy.

He then had to warm her by the stove, rubbing her feet and hands first. Then he rubbed more of her, and the movements of his hands were different. Slower.

He kissed her quite a lot, and she softened, relaxing and moving her hands on him. In contrast, he tightened, trembling and intense. His muscles seemed rigid. Everything on him was hard.

And he took her to the bunk. This time she opened to him shyly, blushing, earnest.

And he loved her. He was gentle and thorough. He rode to her climax and went on to his.

By then, her emotion was such that she cried a little in gasps. He was shocked and knew he'd hurt her, and she had to comfort him.

She was a whole new experience to him. And he was drawn deeper into the net of her. He began to grow more cautious. But she didn't notice and just curled into him and murmured softly how wonderful he was. How marvelous it was that she had met him. How remarkable he was. How loved her body felt. And she made contented sounds as she squirmed closer to him.

He was shocked by his response. It wasn't just wanting her yet again. But it was how it felt to have her curled along him, sighing in contentment, nuzzling her face against him, making sweet sounds of pleasure.

She slept gently. He lay awake, stark eyed, looking at the reflection of the stove on the ceiling. The night fog muffled all sounds so that they seemed alone in the universe.

He looked soberly at the woman next to him, burrowed against him, and her face was beautiful and contented. His arm was under her head and her far shoulder. He curled his hand up along her side and over her sweet breast.

She made a soft, savoring sound in her throat. How could such a lady be such a wanton lover? Such a soft, sweet feast? And again, he felt the thrill of scariness as to what was happening inside him.

The burned log broke in the stove with a soft sound, and she moved in a small surprise. Without thinking, he made a sound in his throat to comfort her. And he felt her relax.

She felt safe in his arms, lying in bed against him. Gently, he kissed her forehead, and his hand moved possessively on her breast and down over her stomach.

She moved her sleeping head against him in a gentle rub of reaction.

Her reaction had been subconscious. She hadn't slept with any other man. Yet she had given him her confidence. He was her protector. It was something he'd never sought. He found it filled him with power.

He could handle anything.

Then he thought of her. That she was far more educated than he. That she was beyond him. And while she slept deeply, her body sated by his, he lay soberly awake.

He was used to waking early. And there she was with her back curled to the front of him. This time, he knew right away who was sleeping with him. He lay, his nose relishing the scent of her. Without her permission, his hands moved on her very sneakily. He wanted her with an intensity that surprised him.

With her eyes closed, she inquired in a whisper, "What is that thumping against my bottom?"

"I suppose I ought to see?" He lifted the blanket from his hot body.

Before he could say anything, she told him, "I think there's a snake in this bed."

"Well... yeah."

"What should I do?"

"It's scared. Could you help it find a place where it'd feel safe?"

Her throaty laugh lifted his hair and shivered his sex.

So it was a while before they had breakfast. He made pancakes. He did a good job of them.

She exclaimed, "You eat something beside chili and rice!"

He opened the food-storage cabinet and showed her pasta, cans of vegetables and meats. Another canned ham. Wieners.

She noted it all and mentioned, "If this fog goes on very much longer, I'll probably have to waddle out of here."

"I'll think of a way you can work off any extra weight."

"Let me guess."

"The floor needs scrubbing."

She laughed so that he laughed along. He'd do anything to keep her from being tired or worried or lonely or anything. He could remember his mother being lonely. She'd cry. How strange to remember that. But she hadn't felt the kids were company. She'd wanted a man.

He could finally sympathize with her. She'd had a rough time. He wondered what had happened to her after she'd taken off.

He looked at Wallis. "You have any sisters or brothers?"

"I have a sister who lives in England."

"Married to a lord."

"How'd you know that?"

"As elegant as you are, your sister would have to be special enough to get a rich man."

"She loved him."

"She would."

Wallis tilted her head and asked, "How could you say that?"

"You're so independent that she probably would be."

"She is. She drives him crazy."

"She makes his life bad?"

"No, she's careless driving her car and meeting people and trying to change the world, and he's scared something could happen to her."

Clint could understand that. He was already worried about the next time Wallis would want to hunt weeds.

And where did he get the sureness that he would control this woman? She had a gun. Not knowing anything about him, she had put the mean gun's snout out the car window, aiming right at his stomach, and she'd said, "Bang!"

She could be a handful.

There sounded a sound. Clint got the communication receiver from its place. Into the speaker, he said, "Yeah?"

It was Lemon this time. "You haven't checked in."

Clint replied, "No reason."

"All's well?"

"Yeah." Clint's reply was rather brief.

"How about the third shift? They get off okay?"

"Yeah."

"Foggy?"

"Yeah."

"I used just one word to show I could do that, too. How's our guest?"

"Here. You can ask her." He handed Wallis the gadget, saying to her, "It's Lemon Covington."

Eight

Clint looked hard at Wallis as he handed her the satellite gadget. She would be talking to Lemon, who was of her kind. She would begin to compare him to Lemon. Clint would lose. Soberly, he listened.

"This is Wallis Witherspoon. Thank you for sending Clint to save me."

Lemon asked, "Did he tell you that?"

"No. He said the dog made him follow."

"That is what happened."

"He's taken good care of me." She looked up and smiled salaciously at her host.

He bit into his lower lip to control his beastly chortle. Then he sat down at the table and began to shuffle the cards . . . as he pretended not to be interested in her conversation.

Wallis said to Lemon, "We've played a lot of double

solitaire. He's had practice." And saying that, she grinned wickedly at her host.

His hands dropped the cards and covered his gasp of shock.

She coughed just a little and said gently, "Your men have all been very courteous. You have a fine crew."

"Thank you. We've found your car. One of the hands was out in the fog and used it for shelter. I'm sorry to say that it's in bad shape. It was really tumbled by the flood."

"What was he doing out?"

"He'd been dropping some raw meat for the puma you found, and his plane sputtered out on him."

"He should have stayed with the plane."

"He did. He came down by the riverbed in a very entertaining way. He'll probably find another means of making a living after his experience."

"I am so sorry. Did he see if the puma was near where he dropped the meat?"

"It was socked in by then. But she didn't bother him."

"Tell him how much we appreciate his helping the puma. That was a fine thing to do."

"Clint advised it. He said she was very thin and had kits."

Wallis put in, "We saw them leave the river bottom."

"Well, that's one worry off our backs." Then Lemon told her, "My love, Renata, and John's wife, Margot, are looking forward to meeting you. So are all the rest of us. I know Clint will get you through about anything. He's a good man."

"Yes," she said softly. "He is."

Lemon added, "If you need anything, holler. We'd find a way to get to you."

"Everything here is just fine."

"Good. Goodbye for now."

"Bye."

Clint took the gadget and turned it off.

Wallis said, "His voice is almost as good as yours."

Clint asked needlessly, "You like the sound of me?"

"Umm."

"Careful, woman, you're being wickedly tempting."

"Just because I said I like the way you sound when you speak?"

"No. It was those sly looks, when you said I was taking good care of you."

She was very, very surprised by his accusation. "I was? Gee. All's I said was just that. You've fed me and kept me warm and given me fascinating instruction in intricate manners."

He laughed and pushed back from the table. "Come sit on my lap."

She lifted her nose snippily. "There're other chairs. You don't have the only one. I can sit by myself."

"Woman! Come here!"

"An . . . order?"

"Please." He smiled at her, so amused.

She put her hands into her free hair and wrapped the hair around her head and allowed it to fall and spring free. She was flirting. Teasing.

He knew that and loved it. He watched her with all his attention.

She wallowed in it.

The radio played an old song with a hard beat. She moved to it in a sassy way, showing him that she was disobeying his command to sit on his lap.

So he reached out and snared her hand to pull her to him.

She pulled back, but was only using the time to move to the music. She jiggled and showed off while she pretended to ignore him. So then she could be very surprised when she found herself on his lap.

"You're a flirt."

"I've never been accused of that before now. How did you decide I was a flirt?"

"You were dancing around, jiggling deliberate."

She protested, "I like music. I was only responding to it."

"And taunting me."

She clasped her hands behind his neck and said, "I wouldn't do a thing like that."

"You need to be careful of me."

"You're a caring man." Her fingers combed his thick hair from his white forehead.

"I saved your hide. What're you gonna do to thank me?"

She sighed with great drama. "That again."

His throat rumbled as he hugged her close, gently rubbing his face against her soft breasts.

"Are you this friendly with all the women you rescue from pumas?"

"You're my first. I wasn't sure how to act, but you've made it easy for me to accept your gratitude."

And she snorted. She rubbed her fingers in his hair, mussing it, and she put her hands on either side to waggle his head as she said, "You!"

"Me...what." It wasn't a question. It was an encouragement for her to talk about him to him.

She laughed and rose from his lap to stand, watching him.

But he was serious. He wanted to hear what she might have to say about him. And he realized that this was the first time he'd ever wondered what a woman really thought about him. That was scary.

She told him, "You are so competent. You can do anything. I've seen you control animals and men in the most unthreatening way. You seem only serious when you push for what you want them to do. So, therefore, you appear logical. What you demand so logically is right. You cook a wonderful meal and you make perfect tortillas. You are respected. I heard Lemon Covington, whom you say is your boss, placate you and allow you to do whatever you choose. He respects you. He gave no orders."

Only then did Clint realize all that she said was true. He was respected.

He said, "When I came with Lemon, when he took over the place some years back, I had to fight just about everybody."

"If that was so, and you had to literally fight your way, the men were not, then, disciplined."

Even then she was right.

She went on thoughtfully, "You probably saved Lemon's hide."

He couldn't drag Lemon down to his level, but he couldn't bear to compliment another man to her at that time. He had to say it, and so he did, "Lemon's a good man."

"I believe it."

But it was insecurity when he blurted, "He treats me like I'm his equal."

"He probably wishes he was like you."

Clint studied her for humor or sarcasm. There was no trace of either. "You're good for my ego."

"You have none."

He had to say it to her. "I'm proud."

"That's acceptable. It's 'ego' that's a no-no."

He frowned a little. "What's the difference?"

As she moved around, she gestured. "Think of the men you know. Some strut and act as if they're superior. Some simply either do a job themselves or see to it that the job is done right."

He recognized himself in the last part. He admitted, "I strut."

"You mostly do it for humor. You are amused by doing it."

"How can you know that?"

"I've been—intimately—involved with you."

He scoffed. "You can tell all that when this is the first time you've had sex?"

"Sex was separate. It's separate, but you're as careful and thoughtful of me as you are of the jobs that must be done. You do it all . . . right. You're a specialist at loving. Someone was very kind to you and taught you well. I'm glad you were my first lover."

"You planning on taking a survey?"

And she laughed. "No."

"Then why did you call me your . . . first?"

"You are!"

His eyes narrowed. "You going around looking for somebody else?"

She folded her arms under her pushy breasts and surveyed the seated Clint. "Not likely. I'm going to try to snare you."

He inquired, "Is a woman supposed to tell a guy that?"

"No. I'm just showing you that I'm being completely honest."

"Aren't you generally?"

Knowing she had all his attention, Wallis looked aside. "Polite is the word, otherwise. When you're being courteous, you don't tell things baldly, you select the facts that are kind."

He considered. "When a woman's cross-eyed and has salt bloat, you tell her she has pretty cheeks?"

"Teaching smoothness to you is like teaching a dog to scratch fleas."

Clint nodded. "But you don't mention the fleas, you just say he's active?"

She sassed. "I won't tell you how to suck eggs."

"So you've heard that one."

Really stretching it, she elaborated with an awful accent, "I've been out in these here parts for quite a spell."

"You're picking up the color."

And she couldn't resist saying, "Sho 'nuff."

"Do I look good to you?"

"I couldn't believe what a wonder you were when you came down that hill on Frankenstein. You were magnificent."

"You was scared spitless and was glad to see anybody."

"How modest. You need to know that I wasn't afraid of you. I didn't wonder if the puma might have been the better choice between you."

"Yeah," he agreed. "I can see that."

"You're very well built. You're a physical man, therefore your muscles are toned well."

"You think I'm stupid?"

"You told Leo how you were going to save my neck, and you did it. You are as sly as a barn cat with three females having litters at the same time."

He exuded maleness. He leaned back in the chair and tilted it onto the back two legs. He said, "Honey, I'm no barn cat."

She smiled patiently, knowingly.

He went on easily, "I'm not a sly barn cat. I'm a very dangerous prairie wolf."

"I have never seen a prairie wolf, but you could be right. You'd be about as easy to catch as one, from what I hear of the creatures."

"You gonna try to catch me." A statement. His eyes narrowed as he considered her.

"You're really an obsolete man."

"Ob-so-leet? Now, how could you say that about a perfectly good, healthy man?"

"I don't mean your time is past. It's your brain—"

"Now, listen here, woman—"

"I'm not insulting your cranial capacity. It's a compliment. You think differently from too many other men, at this time. You see the whole panorama of the interweaving of nature and you dislike disrupting the balance. You're why I was in this part of TEXAS. Yes, I know it's always said or written in capitals."

"You're trainable."

"Even saying that betrays your character. You didn't discard me or threaten me, you think I'm...trainable."

"But you think I'm obsolete."

"Not you, but your kind of man. We need more of you."

He sighed as if it would be very trying and time consuming. "You want me to impregnate the entire female part of TEXAS?"

"Just me."

His foot slipped and his chair came down on all four legs in a bang and his eye crinkles were white. He was shocked. "Do you realize what you're saying?"

"Well, I did catch your attention."

He protested, "I can't be hampered by any excess baggage."

"Is that why men once called women 'baggage'?"

He said, "I wasn't around when that word got started. I'm fairly new and fresh."

"I can attest to the fresh part."

"You're snippy," he chided.

"The word is responsive. I don't make you go alone on the conversational treadmill."

He sorted out her response to verify what she said and he replied, "Thank you."

"You're welcome." She tilted her head as she regarded him. "You and Leo are really very similar."

"You think I'm a—dog?" He was offended.

"No. You're both very caring. He tried his damnedest to figure a way to get me out of that mess and get me past the puma. You realize he understood the puma had kittens? He tried to lure her away, but he didn't harm her."

"She'd have scratched the coat off him."

Wallis agreed. "He really upset her."

"But you weren't upset. You were careful of the cat."

She was curious. "What would you have done in my place?"

"First, I would never have taken a car into that riverbed. Do you know the quicksand down there?"

"There's quicksand?"

"Didn't you notice how carefully we rode Frankenstein?"

"I thought you didn't want to joggle me. But if you *had* been in that place, say, taken there by some dumb woman as you slept in the back seat, what would you have done?"

"Just about what you did. But I'd have undone the door so I could have swung it open, soundlessly, and when she had to nurse the cubs or finally had to find food, I'd have been out of there."

"What if she'd chased you? You're meat, and she was hungry."

"I'd have handled that whatever way it took. There were loose rocks the size to use to knock her out or away. And I would have rolled."

"I had tennis shoes. I believe I'll get boots. Running away, the tennis shoes could have slipped or I could have turned an ankle."

He told her, "You're never going alone again."

"I'm taking along someone to eat?"

He smiled slowly over her words. Then he said, "My lap's empty."

So she filled it.

They wakened for lunch and went out to see if the water supply was adequate for the animals and to inspect the fog.

Neither mentioned the sneaky fact that the fog might be thinning. They rejected that possibility.

They talked all afternoon. They moved to the bunk without mentioning it, and they lay together, talking, telling about themselves and their ideas.

Clint wanted to stay as Lemon's right-hand man. He wanted the expanse of a big spread, and that was the only way to satisfy his ambition to see to land. He didn't have to worry about the finances or the side problems. He just saw to the cattle and the care of the land.

She nodded. "I can see that. To be a part of something important that can make a difference. Are you in politics?"

"Naw. I wouldn't be involved in the government for anything. A life of living in a city and arguing for things would drive me nuts."

"Do you support candidates?"

"Sure. We take them around, and Lemon gives them money."

"Pork-barrel politics?"

"No." He said it kindly and his explanation showed all the things she'd said of him. "We just want to help good men do their jobs. We can handle the ranch."

She smiled blindingly. He'd said what she had wanted to hear. She propped herself up on her elbow and asked, "If I do snare you, will we have any time together? Or will I sit around praying for fog?"

He made a sound in his throat so basic as he put his hand on his chest and rubbed it gently.

"What's the matter?" She asked in quick seriousness.

"You tilt me."

"Bosh."

"If I make love to you again, you might try to escape."

She guessed, "You don't ordinarily have this much free time to spend with a woman?"

"I'd be trying for every spare minute I could find, just to be around you. That's for sure."

"Why?"

"I like hearing you talk and I like looking at you."

"No sex?"

"We can do that anytime, any place."

"Well, I can think of inappropriate times and places. Don't you notice things like that?"

He asked carefully, "Was it...in-ah-pro-pree-ate here?"

"No. This was a miracle! And the fog!" She gestured to the window. "How could I have contrived such a marvelous fog? I'd been praying you'd break your leg."

That shocked him. "You wanted me to break a *leg?*" His voice went up quite high with the last word. "How would you have ever gotten me to the privy?"

"I just thought if you couldn't ride, we'd have to stay here, and it would be nice to get acquainted."

"When you want me to hang around, just mention it and I'll find a way."

She chided, "You haven't kissed me for a long, long time."

His smile came unbidden. He said in a husky voice, "You want some more?"

Prissily, she told him, "I only asked for a kiss. One."

"Yeah, and you know good and well what will happen next."

"How many more condoms do you have?"

He assured her, "Enough."

"I find it very interesting that you carry so many around when you're out, away from the ranch. Do you run across so many willing women?"

"Leo found you. I wasn't even looking. But aren't you glad I had some?"

So, of course, she inquired, "Have you ever used some of your saddle supply?"

"I've given them to some of the men who were off to a town and would probably be horny."

"Then you carry the condoms to protect the men from contacts that could be questionable?"

He agreed. "Mostly."

"And otherwise?"

He considered before he replied. "I must of been antic-i-pating you for some long time. How come it took you so long to get out here where I could find you?"

She became serious. "I know. You scare me a little. What if this is all a dream, and I'm still in that car? I told you I dreamed of being rescued by a man on a black horse. Is this still the dream?"

His voice was foggy as he countered, "You are. God, woman. What are you doing to me?"

"To *you?* What do you mean—to you? I think you've ruined me for any other man! The fog will thin out, we'll go back to civilization. You'll have things you must do. I'll go back to searching for the grasses. And this will all be only a dream."

"Not necessarily." His throat clacked in the stillness. "You have to seriously think about what you're doing to me. You could wreck me, woman. There hasn't been much love in my life. You're taunting me with the idea of it. You're acting like I can mean something to you. You could just be one of those women who need to experience a cowboy. And you think I'm an adventure.''

She was indignant. "Who was the witch who did that to a man like you, if you are actually a real person and not a hunger dream of mine in a stuck car?"

"You're here with me. And I know about user women. I've run into a couple."

"Both sexes have those who are foolers. I'm sorry you had to be hurt by any of my half of the gender gap."

He asked carefully, "Are you a . . . fem-i-nist?"

"Probably."

"Think what our daughters will be like."

She smiled with his unconscious commitment. "Our daughters will take after you. They'll prowl the prairie."

"I'll keep them under my thumb."

She considered him. "You would, too. And you'd be very sure your sons knew how to handle anything."

"I'd try...for you. For your approval. I'd care what you thought of me as a man...and as the father of your babies."

"Is this going fast for you, too?"

His reply was slow but thoughtful and completely honest. "We've gotten a lot of important things gone through. We know each other better than most couples after years."

And she was sobered by his evaluation. "You could be right." It hadn't just been chatter. They'd exchanged very serious testings and ideas. It had been unusual.

His voice still foggy, he said, "I'm trying to think of a way to keep you here with me."

"I'd probably want other clothes besides borrowed long johns and whoever's shirt, plus my own slacks and shirt."

"So you're a picky woman."

"Probably. I'd like to reach current newspapers. What happened nine months ago is, to quote a quote, old news."

"We have the radio."

"No TV."

"Oh-oh, now we're getting down to basics."

"You don't watch television?"

"Yep. And we get all the tapes."

"Glory be!"

"See? You won't miss a thing. Do you know...now listen to this—CNN has come out here to film *us!*"

"Well, how about that! Why?"

And Clint laughed. "You don't think we're—uh—on the cutting edge?"

She said airily, "Not particularly. You still ride horses."

"Riding horses is a lost art."

"Wow! Where'd you get the wordage?"

His eyes spilled humor. "Peter Jennings was here, once."

"Why did he come here?"

"You doubt my—uh—revelation?"

"No. I just wondered what brought him out this way."

"We had one hell of a blizzard and we were trying to keep the cattle from piling up. It fascinated Peter. He's a good reporter."

She grinned. "He helped with the cattle?"

"He directed the cameramen. I have a copy of the tape. On a hot July afternoon, I'll show it to you. Man, it was cold enough to freeze . . . a body. If you watched it in winter, you'd get a serious chill."

"I'm cold just thinking about it."

He got up and put more wood on the stove. Then he gathered the things for their dinner.

They did biscuits again. He guided her through the process, and it worked again. He made a few tortillas on the side to eat with cheese melted in the middle of the rolled round bread substitute.

They had a home-canned stew that was perfect.

She sopped up some of the gravy and said, "Who made this?"

"He's a personal friend of Lemon's and he's this good with other foods. He's got his own canning equipment. Pretty good, huh?"

"If I stay with you, do you keep on with the cooking, or do you expect me to learn to compete with this friend of Lemon's?"

His voice went husky again. "I'd just want you on a silk cushion looking pretty for me."

She was appalled. "Here I am, you've said the perfect lure, and I didn't have a tape recorder!" In elaborate anguish, she put her hands into her hair.

He grinned and then laughed. "But I did say it, and you liked it."

"Since we don't have any tape recorders, what do you want me to say to you that I could get away with saying?"

"That you could love me."

She looked at him and her face became serious. "Clint, I believe I could. It scares me considerably."

"Me, too."

"We need to see each other under more normal circumstances."

Earnestly, he promised, "We will. We'll be serious about this. I can't believe you want to talk to me and test me when you already have tasted me."

She laughed and put her hands over her pink face. "That was scandalous."

He shook his head slowly, his eyes never leaving hers. "It was heaven."

"You're not very demanding. Are you easy with me because you want to lure me in, for now? Then, you'll spring all sorts of quirks and demands that I can't meet, and you'll be free of me?"

"Is that the way you'd be with me?"

"I doubt it very seriously. While these are very limited circumstances, you've handled yourself superbly. All I have to see is how crazy you are around some fantastic woman. You've admitted to being a prairie wolf."

He was sure. "Us prairie wolves are selective."

"I've read recently that some of the dominant female's pups don't have the dominant male's DNA."

"No!" He was greatly shocked. "Is that why they're called bitches?"

Scandalized, she responded, "I just wonder."

And he laughed.

She watched him as she smiled. Then she asked, "Want some dessert?"

"My choice?"

"There's canned pudding, canned cookies, more coffee or hot chocolate."

"I want you."

"I'm not sure I can again, this soon."

He was silent for a minute; then he suggested kindly, "You can hum and look out the window."

She got up and went at him to ruffle his hair.

But he easily caught her forearms, turned her and there she was, back on his lap.

He nuzzled and kissed, and his hands roamed around in a very tender way. She made sounds of pleasure and moved so that she was more available to his exploration. Then her clothing was shifted, so she rearranged his. She said she was just seeing to it that he was treated separately but equally.

She made him laugh.

Somehow they got over to the bunk and darned if he didn't make love to her again. They were voluptuous and steamy and slow. They moved and slid and rubbed together.

She gasped and squeaked and moaned. She was intense and invited all sorts of liberties and helped.

He groaned and said sweet words, and in their throes, the name he said was hers.

Sometime later, they did remember to go out and see the animals.

It was with inner grief that they saw the fog was lifting.

How could it.

Nine

Again, Clint and Wallis shared the same bunk that night. They slept lightly and wakened often to find each other and rearrange themselves to be closer. And their touches were almost nostalgic. Yearning. Scared?

With first morning light, they lay side by side, holding hands.

Finally Wallis said, "You look. I haven't the heart to see it."

He lay silently. "I can see, right now, that I'm gonna get all the dirty jobs... changing the kids, stoking the fires on cold mornings...."

"Probably."

He rolled over and kissed her in a soft, brief salute. Then he got out of bed and went to the door. He did it so that she would be able to see for herself. He opened it.

The fog was a wall that instantly collapsed inside the door.

He laughed. He turned back to look at her across the room, and they both just laughed.

He closed the door and went back to bed to nuzzle her and rub his morning whiskers on her throat.

In a foggy voice, he told her, "I've got to quit kissing you, or they'll all know what I've been doing to you."

"What have you done to me?"

So he had to show her. He complained the whole, entire time about the burden put upon him because she had no memory at all.

She would say, "I don't remember you doing that!"

And he'd have to repeat it, as he explained when he'd done it. She was disbelieving, and he'd have to do it again!

He said she was a slow learner and had a faulty memory.

So she asked, "About what?"

She had made him laugh, yet again. He warned her seriously, "You could ruin me for any other woman."

"I'm trying."

Lazily, he asked, "You acting another way than you really are?"

"No. This is the real Wallis Witherspoon."

"Tell me about your family."

"I have a perfectly good mother and father and one sibling. But not too many kinfolk. They're all pleasant and politely interested, if you insist on their attention. I've always longed for a brother."

He sighed and shook his head as he admitted, "I'm sure 'nuf not the brotherly type."

"I recognized that almost right away, after I realized you probably weren't a gunrunner."

"A . . . *gun*runner?" His disbelieving voice squeaked upward.

"Or a coyote—the kind who smuggles aliens into the country."

"They are a problem, but you have to know we don't cotton to that kind of thing? People pay money to be smuggled into this country and end up dead, smothered in the airless trunks or lost in the brush, dying of thirst."

She shook her head slowly as she frowned.

Then he asked in curiosity, "Why would you think I was a gunrunner?"

"You looked dangerous. You were on a horse, so you could sneak around and not be seen on roads. And you came down that bank like a man who could handle anything. I didn't understand, right off, that you were a prairie wolf, until you most kindly pointed that out to me."

He commented, "You're getting into the rhythm of the TEXAS language."

"Glad you noticed."

"Will you stick around at Lemon's for a while so's we can test this . . . attraction?"

"You like sex?"

"I want to see if we can get along when we're not in bed."

"Me, too. Will Lemon mind if I stay around? Is there a place for me to stay that isn't too far from—"

"There's room at Lemon's. You'll stay there."

"I can't stay in your room, with you."

"Sure you can."

"No. I'd be embarrassed. Are there hotels or motels around somewhere?"

"You can have your own room at Lemon's."

"You're sure I wouldn't be intruding?"

"They love company," he assured Wallis. "There're almost always strangers or friends staying around, and Lemon says it's good for the house crew to have the steady work. They could get lazy and spoiled."

"I'm looking forward to meeting them."

"They're lucky to have the chance."

She smiled at him. Then she asked, "Is there a car dealership anywhere close? I'm . . . afoot."

"We'll figure it out."

She stretched luxuriously and said, "Breakfast in bed?"

He piled the pillows behind his head and said, "Well, okay. I want—"

She explained to him, "*You're* the cook!"

"Uh, oh. I can see a flaw! Who'd think a friendly woman like you could turn— Now wait a minute, there, woman! Let's get this straightened out!"

He pinned her as she laughed and squirmed. Then he kissed her and shifted her around until she was on top of him, and he held her with cherishing. He said, "You scare the hell out of me."

"Because I want breakfast in bed?"

"Because you might disappear."

"I wish I had that on tape, then I could play it for you when you're saying I ought to get along and go on home."

"Do you suppose we could come to that?"

She smiled down into his eyes and said, "We'll find out."

He hugged her to him and groaned. He asked, "How can we fix breakfast locked together thisaway?"

They kissed gently. But when she rubbed her face against his, he stopped her. With tender concern, he told her, "You're getting whisker burned."

She appeared shocked and asked, "Where?"

It took him some time to indicate all the places on her, and breakfast was again delayed.

The only reason they got up at all was that Leo scratched on the door and said, *"Wuff."*

Clint explained, "That means 'breakfast' and we're late with it."

She guessed, "He uses *wuff* because he wuffs it down?"

"I never thought of it thataway. I had supposed it was just a dog sound."

"Some people are insensitive."

And Clint laughed. He got up, holding her against his front, and still holding her with his arms tightly around her, he walked that way to the door.

He released one hand from her and opened the door. Leo stood there patiently, and Clint asked, "What'd ya want, boy?"

And again the dog explained, *"Wuff."*

Wallis laughed, her whisker-reddened face beautiful under her dark, tousled, ducktailed hair.

So the dog came inside, out of the fog and flopped down on the rug.

Clint carried his woman against his front over to the counter and set her up on it. Sitting there, she gave him kisses as he demanded them, while he opened a can of dog food . . . with his knife, of course.

He put the food in a mixing bowl and put it down on the floor. It was what the dog waited for, and he ate.

Wallis said she was going out to the privy. She called it the outhouse. Clint's word was neither one, and he didn't mention what he called it.

Leaving her sitting on the counter, Clint got her shoes, banged them against his foot to empty any lurking scorpions and helped her put them on and tie them. Then he lifted her down from the counter, but he took a long time in the doing of it, inching her down his body.

She smiled the entire time. And being a strong man, he resisted adding to her whisker burn.

When she returned to the shack, he was in jeans and stirring a grain-mix cereal with raisins, dried apples and date pieces. It was served with canned milk. And there was the pot of coffee, fresh and filling the shack with the fragrance.

It was strong coffee.

Wallis took a sip and then considered the cup. She said thoughtfully, "I am surprised it doesn't eat through."

"A rat?" He looked around, listening.

"There are . . . rats?"

"Probably. What were you talking about?"

"The coffee in my cup."

Deliberately sober faced, he lectured her, "That is not your personal cup. It's a shack cup. You can't take it away with you. You have to leave it here."

"Oh."

"I'm glad we got that straightened out before we left. I understand how people in strange places—or is it strange people in places? I think it was people in strange places, I'll have to check my notes." He went on eating.

"What about strange people in places?"

Without looking up, he said, "You gotta leave the cup here."

"I wasn't showing attachment to the cup, I was—"

"You're attached to me."

And she said, "Not right now. I'm sitting alone over here, on my chair and I'm amazed the coffee isn't eating through this cup."

"It might not be hungry... and you can't own the chair."

She lifted her eyebrows a fraction and responded, "I hadn't considered that."

He *tsked*. "You wicked woman. You're luring me with nonsense."

"No. I'm serious. This coffee is strong."

He sipped his own. Then he sipped hers. And he had the gall to explain patiently, "The coffee in one cup is like the coffee in another."

Then she protested, "Of *course* it's the same! It's from the same pot!"

"Well, I'll be darned."

People in love can find odd things fascinating. The rest of the morning went along in variations of the same way.

At noon, the fog had lifted back. So they reluctantly got Frankenstein out of the shed and cleared it neatly; then they mounted the horse and went out toward the river. He showed her the compass.

She exclaimed, "I believed you could see your way!"

He was indignant. "You were *supposed* to."

"Are you sure you're not a sly coyote?"

"I never lie."

She hugged his back. She only felt his strength, she wasn't really aware of how his back could feel her body, her softness, the differences of her.

Over the river, the fog was thick enough they could alibi out another day. So they went back to the shack.

Down from the horse, she danced before the cabin, exuberantly. She said, "It's like having a snow day from school!"

He told her, "We get snow here, on occasion. It's a real nuisance."

She was still dancing and turning around, her arms out and up and swinging, showing off for him. She opened her arms out to the fogged sky and cried out, "I *love* fog!"

He stood with one hand on his pistol butt and said, "You're strange."

And she made a disparaging sound.

He commented idly, "It's just probably a good thing that I'll have to make our living. I could just shack up with you for the rest of my life."

"Do you know how to deliver babies?"

"I've delivered just about everything else, but I do admit I've never delivered a real human baby."

She grinned and looked at him from the corners of her eyes as she turned, showing off, and she advised, "Practice."

He went to her and stopped her so that he could hug her. He did that as if he never had before right that minute. He groaned over the wonder of her.

She knocked off his hat, which was so precious that he put it on before he dressed in the morning, and she said, "You act as if you've never had a woman so close at hand before now."

His emotion-fogged voice told her the truth. "I've never been so taken with a woman. You scare me. Maybe we've really met in your dreams—and this will all . . . disappear."

She looked around with perky interest. "I would have dreamed a better house . . . with indoor plumbing."

His face buried against the side of her throat, he stated an opinion. "Spoiled."

They got back on Frankenstein and left the cabin to go farther away from the river. The fog thinned enough to get bearings, and he still carried the compass. They allowed Frankenstein to set his own pace, and Leo trotted along beside them. He was glad to be out and about.

They went out onto the flat heights. There, they could look over the distance and the fog hung like smoke, covering all the hollows.

The sky was still filled with low, soft, smoky-colored clouds. The four spectators, who were isolated viewers, seemed sandwiched between two lands. They occupied a mid-way place of nothingness. But it wasn't depressing or lonely. They had each other, and at that time no need or longing for anyone else.

When he spoke, she knew he felt the same strangely magical isolation. "Will it always be this way?"

She replied, "I think the time will come when we willingly allow others inside."

And he smiled because their thinking was in sync.

With Frankenstein cropping along, his reins trailing, and Leo off within what he considered a whistle distance, the two lovers walked hand in hand in their strange magic nowhere.

While he allowed her to kiss him anywhere she liked, and he returned her kisses, he wouldn't allow nor did he touch her face. He got some awful smelling ointment from his saddlebag and smeared it on her face quite lavishly.

She sputtered and spat and objected.

It did stink. It was for cattle.

To share her discomfort, he put it on him, too, in earnest compassion, but he said, "I can't have you turning up among strangers, with me, and you be whisker burned."

With squint-eyed retaliation in mind, she said, "Let's let your beard grow, and I'll pluck it bare."

"Wow! Revenge?"

She smiled. "Yeah."

"You terrify me."

She grinned, then she sobered gently and said, "I could be hampering. You need to be sure. You're right to take this slow."

"I'm only thinking of you."

"You need to take some consideration for yourself. I am a different woman. Emotionally, I could throw you for a loop."

He watched her for a minute, then he said softly, "I'm not an ordinary man."

"That was apparent when you came down that bank, then hollered like an attacking Comanche and recklessly intruded into an upset puma's territory."

"I *was not* reckless! I knew exactly what to do, what Frankenstein would do and what Leo would do. I even knew what the *puma* would do. The only iffy one in the bunch was you!"

It was revealing, then, that she should laugh and her eyes would twinkle delightfully.

And even more revealing was that he pulled her into his arms and kissed her, ointment and all.

When he lifted his head from hers, her eyes were heavy lidded and her mouth swollen from his attention. She moved her lips to say, "I thought you'd given up on kissing me."

"You get sassy, and I can't help it."

"So," she commented. "It's my fault."

"Yeah."

"We need to discuss responsibilities."

To that, he immediately replied, very seriously, "I'll support you."

"Not that. You said I shouldn't go back whisker burned, you slathered that stinky junk all over me and then you just went ahead and kissed me again."

"Your fault."

"See? You need to learn to accept the responsibility for your own acts."

So he laid her on the ground and made love to her in that strange land between high fog and low clouds. It was a mating as it must have been for the old gods. It was cosmic.

As they lay replete, she asked, "Will we survive in ordinary life?"

And he assured her, "Yes."

"You are real?"

He replied emphatically, "Painfully."

"I'm afraid."

"How could you be afraid of me, when you weren't afraid of a puma?"

"A puma is a pussycat compared to you. You could rip me apart."

He was shocked. "I wouldn't hurt you, Wallis. How could you think that?"

"If I'm snared and you'd leave me, you would rip out my heart."

With slow seriousness, he replied, "You'd still have mine, and you'd survive."

"We ought to be more careful. This is getting scary."

He eased from her, shifted off her and sat up, his clothes still askew. He rubbed his face with both hands, then sat with his arms on his knees and his hands hanging down.

She sat up slowly, next to him and she was very quiet. She looked around again at the cloud Valhalla. But they were alone.

Was this a testing of a new experiment by the gods? How could they know? They were mortal. She was. She asked, "Have you mingled with the old gods?"

"Only just in the last few days."

Then she smiled. She shifted her bottom over so that she was alongside him but facing the other way. She laid her head against his shoulder, and he laid his head on hers.

They were filled with wonder and an amazing peace. Nothing could touch them.

But they were human. They became aware that time was passing and they needed to get back. He put her on his horse and stood a minute just to see her there. She looked back. It was an intense exchange. It was important.

Then he got into the saddle, sliding his leg forward to avoid her body, and he whistled for Leo.

Leo came loping along until he was in sight and seen; then he waited. He was indicating they should stay on the high, flat land as long as they could. It was logical, and Clint followed the dog who took them back to the shack.

The dog did that. Of course, Clint was aware and checked the compass, but the dog knew his way. And it was to that shack.

As Clint lifted her down from Frankenstein, she asked, "Did he ever live here?"

"Only in the last few days."

"But he was here before then?"

"Maybe with Lemon, in those days before I came back to the place and Leo recognized me."

"Can we buy him from Lemon?"

Very carefully, Clint told her, "The dog chose me. He's mine, the way Frankenstein is, and the way you are."

"I rank right up there with—"

"Wallis! You know what I mean. You are more important than any animal or any human. I don't know why it's that way, but it is."

"I was teasing you."

He took the key down and unlocked the door. He checked out the room before he opened the door for her to go inside. He said, "Okay. But you need to know exactly how I take you."

"I've experienced that several times now."

"Don't get mouthy."

"I love you."

He asked rather roughly, "Are you trying to—soothe me?"

She went to the sink and pumped some water. "Not in the least. I just mentioned that I love you as well as either Leo or..."

He hung his hat on one of the pegs. "Am I going to hear about this for the rest of our lives?"

She gave him a cup of water. Then, snootily, she confirmed it. "It just might come in handy here and there along the way."

"I just might have to take another look at you."

"You do that. But I must tell you this encounter with you has been amazing. I've never felt this way before, and you are a very skilled lover. Now, let's quarrel."

"About what?"

"Are we so new that we have no bones to gnaw on? How about—"

"If you say one word, I'll walk."

"Off? Just like that?"

"No. Outside, back and forth."

"A threat!"

And he laughed. "You're impossible."

"I've proven this entire time that I'm very possible. And you've taken full advantage of the premise."

"If I find I want to get rid of you, how am I going to do it, if you go on making me laugh?"

"We won't quarrel. My grandmother told a story from her grandmother. She said a farm couple decided they'd never quarrel. If she was angry and touchy, she'd tuck up her apron. Her husband could see the wisdom of that. He decided if he was touchy, he'd put his hat on the back of his head. So as they went along, if she had her apron tucked up, he would be quiet and helpful, and if his hat was on the back of his head, she would do the same. But one day he came home with his hat on the back of his head and found her with her apron tucked up."

"What happened?"

"I don't know. The story ended there." She considered. "I suppose all hell broke loose."

He suggested, "Or maybe she was like you, and she made him laugh?"

"You get mad pretty easily."

Clint chided, "You were lining yourself up as being equal with a dog and a hor—"

"Well, at *least* that muc—"

Warningly, he cautioned, "Wallis!"

But she laughed.

He said thoughtfully, "I might get used to you."

"You'll probably have the time."

"I'll make it."

She asked, "To live with me? Or to save yourself *from* me?"

"Both. But I meant that I'd make the time to do a good study of you and teach you to obey and straighten up."

She straightened until just the hard nipples showed under her shirt. "Straightened up, like that?"

"I may never live long enough to find out."

"Why?" She went in back of him, curled close against him, running her hands down his front.

"I've forgotten."

She scolded, "You're susceptible."

"I've noticed that very thing." He could feel the chuckle in her body. Then he told her, "Wallis, don't underestimate how much I'm taken with you. Don't belittle how I feel."

"You will tell me on occasion?"

"All the time," he promised.

"You really don't need to ever tell me. Just treat me that way."

"I do love you." He shook his head once.

She lay her cheek on his back and asked, "Is that head shake a rejection?"

"It's wonder. I never expected to find you."

They had supper and went to bed. While he was careful not to let his beard touch her face, his kisses were so consuming that her lips were swollen and scarlet.

The next morning they could see the shed, and a light wind was blowing the fog away. They looked at each other sadly.

Leo and Frankenstein were fed first. The pair of humans knew their strange interlude was over. What would happen to them? When they got back into a regular routine, would their attraction survive? Or was this just a chance interlude that they should allow to fade into memory?

They didn't talk but in soft, occasional exchanges. Both appeared distracted, their minds not there. They tidied the cabin and washed their dishes.

While Wallis swept out the cabin, Clint cleaned out the shed and the privy. He came back and washed his hands in the sink. He saw that she was ready. He also saw that her lips were still puffed and very red. He watched her, not speaking, as she looked in the fogged mirror by the door.

She asked, "Is that what they mean by a scarlet woman?"

"By the time we get to the place, your lips will be like always."

"I still smell of liniment."

"We'll say it was sore muscles?"

She thought on it and said, "Maybe not."

"How about my jerking you wrong when I pulled you out of the puma's jaws?"

"That's pretty good."

"We do need to say the same thing. If you say one way and I say another, everybody will know what we've been doing."

She laughed.

He stood watching her do that, and his smile came slowly and wonderfully. He said, "I do believe I love you, Wallis Witherspoon."

"I quite possibly return that emotion, kind sir."

They stood in the door and looked back into the room, and to the bunk they'd shared. He put his arm around her and hugged her to his side.

She lay her head against him and sighed. "I want to stay here."

"While I could use this shack as home base and make a living with a beef herd, I can't limit you that much. You'd get bored by the second month. You're too sassy and smart to be isolated from other people. You admitted being so picky that you want to read or see current news. And you'd want indoor plumbing."

She took a deep breath and said, "Yeah." But it was a forlorn word.

He turned her to him and hugged her with entrapping arms. He groaned and said, "Don't tempt me."

"Maybe Lemon will let us use the shack now and then, when it isn't needed by the hands."

"I'll ask."

"I've been very careful not to call you dear or darling, because it could become a habit and I could embarrass you in front of your friends, but I want to call you darling now. My darling."

Her eyes were full of tears! And he was almost wrecked. He hugged her closely and kissed her tenderly, and they were delayed leaving.

Frankenstein was frisky, and Leo was very patient and enduring. It was almost noon when they got to the river. The water was muddy. The fog was patchy, but they could see well enough. The flow of water was still higher than normal. However, it was down enough that they could cross cautiously.

While it was a regular cattle crossing, it wasn't a road, and Clint put Wallis down on the bank. Clint stripped Frankenstein of the saddle and blanket and carefully rode him bareback across the river. Clint had to be sure Wallis would be safe crossing. A gully washer could dig out surprise holes in the riverbed, causing a horse to flounder.

He looked back, expecting to see Wallis waiting for him with Leo at her side. Were they? No. Leo was off investigating God only knew what all, and Wallis was picking weeds.

He rode Frankenstein back across the river. Since Clint had to wait until Wallis got several more varieties of weeds, he had enough time to resaddle the horse.

Then he had to whistle for Leo, who was damned independent. And with the whistle for the dog, Clint caught his woman's attention and she finally came to him.

He took his foot from the stirrup. Then he reached down to take her opposite arm and helped her to mount in back of him. Leo watched with enough interest. Then Clint started down the bank as he looked carefully upstream. The muddy water was placid. They went into it carefully and crossed with no problem.

Ten

————

As Frankenstein carried a very quiet and sober-faced Clint and Wallis farther and farther from Paradise, the satellite gadget made its gentle sound.

It was Lemon's voice. "All okay?"

Sparsely, Clint replied, "Fog up, river down, we're on our way in."

"Welcome home."

And instead of clicking off at that time, considering the exchange was complete, Clint said, "Thanks."

At the house, Lemon's finger hesitated over the disconnecting button before very slowly touching it. With his finger still on the button, he stood lost in thought. Then he went in search of Renata.

On a place as large as Lemon's, a line shack was at a distance from the house and from any other line shack. That was the purpose of them: to be available for men a long way from the main buildings and the house.

With all the movement of drifting people who wanted to be somewhere else, the hands never knew what they would find when they went to one of the line shacks. Strangers used and ripped off the shacks repeatedly. So what was stocked was sparse.

There was a helicopter crew that checked the shacks, replenished them and replaced the laundry. Lemon said the men were spoiled rotten. And the men replied, no wonder his name was Lemon. He was a sour man.

As Clint and Wallis went toward the house, Clint held Frankenstein to a walk. Clint considered how he dreaded to have his time alone with her, end.

In another place than his own, among people who were polished, Clint would show up as the rough man he really was. How could he stand beside Lemon and look good to her? He was anguished. It was a new and terrible feeling.

That in his thinking, Clint referred to Wallis only as "her" was very telling. There was no other "her" in his mind.

It was almost suppertime when Clint walked Frankenstein up to the front steps of the center porch at Lemon's place. Clint had done that deliberately, because he didn't want Wallis to go in a back door. To put her down on the front steps was important to Clint.

Wallis accepted it as normal.

She was elegant and perfectly comfortable in her rumpled clothing and tennis shoes. Her hair was an untidy cloud of black ducktails. While her face no longer looked abraded, her lips were still puffy and redder than they should have been.

Swinging his leg forward, Clint got off the horse. Then he turned and reached up his hands to lift her down. Wallis smiled at him and turned her upper body to slide sideways, reaching for his shoulders so that his hands caught her at her waist.

Wallis smiled into his eyes, then lifted her gaze to look beyond as people came from the house onto the porch.

As Clint set her on her feet in front of him, her smile widened. Since her attention had left him, Clint turned to follow the direction of her gaze.

Coming out through the front door, the greeting committee consisted of Lemon and his Renata. And Lemon's live-in financial adviser, John Brown, with his wife, Margot. They came forward, giving greetings and comments and welcomings. Their words warmed Clint's hard heart.

Lemon asked Clint, "Will you allow Peanut to take care of Frankenstein?"

"Yeah."

So Lemon went to the porch edge and put his fingers in his mouth to whistle. Then he came back to share in the introductions.

Clint saw his friends from another point of view. They were charming, practiced hosts. They were being comfortably welcoming to his love.

One of the stablehands came a-running. Clint told him, "Take Frankenstein to Peanut...personal."

And the lackey said, "Right."

Then Clint added a questioning statement, "Give Leo a bath before he comes into the house?"

And the kid grinned and said, "Yes, sir."

Wallis called, "Wait. My specimens."

That made them all curious. And she retrieved her weeds from where she'd stuck them, between the saddle and the saddle blanket.

The weeds intrigued them. Lemon said, "You interested in the primal growth?"

Wallis replied, "All growth. I'm a horticulturist."

Lemon exclaimed, "You're hired! We need you here."

Wallis grinned, but didn't ask if he was serious. She allowed the opening to pass by her. She handled it well.

They were all interested in her "adventure," as they called it. It was John who told them, "When Ben was out today, he saw the puma and her cubs. She'd found the meat."

Clint said, "I thought he'd wrecked the plane."

John explained, "Ben did a really fine job landing that plane as well as he did. It's been dismantled and is being brought back to be fixed."

Renata told Wallis, "I'm impressed you would be out alone. Aren't you scared to go out and about?"

Clint said, "She has the ugliest gun I've ever seen. She could have shot that puma any time and gotten away, but she said only the puma was endangered."

And Margot said, "Great!" She grinned and lifted her fist up to hold it above her head in a salute to courage.

Wallis looked around and said, "What a great porch."

"Would you like to freshen up?" Renata asked. "We're so glad to see you safe again that we're forgetting you may be tired."

It was Wallis who smiled at Renata and replied, "We've had it fairly leisurely with the fog and all. Even today, riding double, we took it easy."

Clint reminded the listeners that they hadn't been alone all the time out at the shack. "The men were sure glad to have the shack in the rain, so they could get dry and sleep. They were so tired, they weren't very good company."

"Was it hard to get Wallis out of the trapped car?"

She immediately replied, "Clint was superb! You should have seen him coming down that bank on Frankenstein!"

While the men smiled, the women's response was serious. The men thought of the adventure and rescue, and the women thought of the danger and entrapment . . . alone.

Wallis was saying, "He lifted me up on Frankenstein's back. Then he had to rescue Leo from the puma! It was exciting! He turned the horse and shot his gun into the air and gave the rebel yell as he pretended to charge the puma. *And she stood her ground,* snarling and furiously scared. But Leo got away. Clint swerved aside from the puma, and we went off along the riverbed. It was really something."

Lemon smiled at Clint.

Margot cheered, indicating Clint, "Again, the hero."

And Clint bowed his head so that his Stetson hid his face as he said, "Shucks, ma'am, 'tweren't nothing."

The laughing couples moved inside, and Margot took Wallis upstairs to a room to freshen up. They were close in size, and Margot brought clothes to Wallis's room for her to choose something fresh.

Renata came along and said, "You will stay with us? There's a phone there by the bed, if you need to call anyone to tell them where you are. The Cactus Ridge address and number are on the phone."

They showed her the bath and said they'd be by to fetch her to supper, if Clint was involved and couldn't take her down himself. He would be along directly. Supper was in about forty-five minutes.

Then they left her alone. She made her phone calls, showered and dressed in Margot's gown. Her hair was blow-dried, and the donated makeup was really excellent. With tender thought to the man responsible, she slathered on quite a bit of cream to soothe her nicely healing face.

She looked in the mirror and smiled as she thought of Clint seeing her in something appropriate for a change.

Predictably, it was Clint who came for her. He was shaved and changed into clothing that was a surprise to her. He'd always looked so rough.

With tender huskiness, he said, "You clean up pretty good."

She smiled and replied, "So do you! Wow! Women must be deeper around you than I first thought."

"What made you think women might be around me?"

"You acted like being around me was easy."

He asked, "Men been careful-er of you than I was?"

"Obviously."

He asked, "Is that makeup manproof? Can I give you a careful kiss?"

"Let's find out."

He took her into his arms and just hugged her as he groaned. "How will I sleep without holding you?"

"We'll think of something."

"You wouldn't mind?"

"Not if we can be discreet, enough."

"I love you, Wallis."

"I'm so glad."

They went down the stairs hand in hand, not talking, and they fooled no one.

With the weather and flooding being as it had been, there were no guests, so it was only the six of them at a much shortened table in the big dining room.

The talk, unsurprisingly, turned to Wallis's reason for being in the area, and then to an intense discussion of grasses.

The three men and Wallis were involved. Margot and Renata listened, and it was interesting to them. They did understand.

But their meal was eaten without real attention to the carefully prepared foods.

At one point, Wallis got up and went to her room to bring back some sample grasses she'd gathered as she'd waited for Clint to test the river crossing.

Lemon was astonished she'd gotten one of them at the river crossing?

She had, and there were more of the strain.

It was interesting to her that Clint had other names for the same grasses. They were cowboy names.

Lemon said, "I was along there in that area not long ago. How could I have missed seeing them?"

"You were looking for something else?" That was Renata, a poet who could be distracted very easily from just about everything but Lemon.

At another time, the women warned Wallis, "Don't try the pinto. If you can ride him, you'll be stuck with training him."

She replied, "I'm a city girl. I've never learned to ride anything enough to train it."

Humor flickered in their eyes, but neither woman commented.

Clint seemed to have extra time because he spent several days showing Wallis around the place. The first of those days, he led her to a very sassy convertible that was really, really red with a white top.

It was his.

She wasn't surprised he'd like such a car, but she had trouble adjusting herself to the fact that Clint Terrell would even *have* a car!

That surprised him. "How did you think I'd get around in this country?"

"I probably could accept you flying, before I'd think you'd run around in such a little fireball."

"You think I'm too old?"

"No. Not old. Just really a horse man."

"I've always had cars. They go faster than horses."

"You need a station wagon."

"A...station wagon?" His tone was stricken.

But she just grinned.

So Lemon and John cornered Wallis with Clint some days later and gave her a serious offer to stay and work for the ranch.

She immediately thought of the difficult pinto and replied, "I can't ride a horse well enough."

Clint was blank, but John laughed and Lemon said, "It's the weeds."

Rather sassily, she instructed, "We call them grasses."

Lemon coaxed nicely, "Help us to find and nurture them. Stay here."

She looked at Clint. He smiled, so he wasn't opposed. He was being careful not to urge her. It had to be her decision.

She needed to talk to Clint, in order to be sure he wouldn't be uncomfortable with her around. So she said, "Let me think about it a while."

And they agreed she had whatever time she might need. But they named a salary that was more than generous.

That night as they crawled into her bed, she asked Clint, "Would it be uncomfortable for you if I stayed and worked here?"

"I've been holding my breath ever since Lemon asked me the first night."

"You didn't say anything to me!"

"Well, those first nights, you distracted me so I just about forgot about it."

"How?"

"Well, now, buttercup, how could you not understand something so simple? Do I have to do it *every* single night?"

"Oh. That."

"Don't make it sound like nothing. Making love to you is heaven for me. Don't you like it very much? I know—"

"I *love* it, and it scares me you could get bored with me. Okay. That's enough. It wasn't meant to be funny. Do you want me to tickle you and give you cause to giggle that way? I'll just—"

And she did try, but he turned her wrestling into something else entirely. And even though they didn't laugh, after a while it was more fun.

He told her, "I like your smell." And he nuzzled around.

She sighed and corrected in a distracted manner, "Fragrance."

About the first thing Wallis did after being hired, was to go with her female cohorts to San Antonio and shop for suitable clothing. Neither comrade mentioned most of Wallis's purchases were underwear and nightwear. But the two exchanged glances of understanding. And they bought some themselves.

The first party the Covingtons gave for Wallis was right after that, and they wore evening attire.

Looking perfect in formal clothing, Clint came down the stairway from the third floor and tapped on Wallis's door. She came to her door and opened it a crack, looking both ways to be sure she wasn't going to shock anyone else. She wore a new sheer negligee. It was flesh colored and didn't hide any colors on her.

Clint gasped and said something he'd never before said seriously, "Why, Wallis Witherspoon! You are a scandal!" And he was shocked.

"I know. It's deliberate. I'm getting used to it, so I can flirt when I wear it for you."

He put his hand to his forehead and staggered to the hall wall for support. He wasn't entirely kidding. He was shocked.

She whispered, "I'm not ready. Go ahead. I'll see you downstairs."

"I could watch." Then he frowned and ran his hand over himself as he said, "Maybe not."

"You go ahead. I'm a little nervous."

"You're not going to wear just . . . that, are you?" And he frowned at her.

"Why?"

"Well, honey, you see it's... I can see...everything."

"Are you that quick? You only got a peek."

"Men know when to look fast at a woman, before she knows what she's doing."

"How wicked." She stared at him. "Go ahead. I'll be down shortly."

Very seriously he urged, "I'd better check you out before you go public."

"My dress is perfectly decent. This is a negligee."

"You just wear it in your room?"

She nodded. "Or yours."

"It does seem that I ought to be able to get used to you." His sun squint lines were white.

"You will. Probably. More than likely. I'll help you."

"Yeah. Behave. Don't surprise me no more until I tell you it's okay."

"Yes, sir."

"Respect is an aphrodisiac."

She gasped, "Why, how shocking! I hadn't known. Sorry."

Soberly, he slowly shook his head. "You got a whole lot to learn."

"Could you wait until after the party?"

"I just hope it won't be too late."

So Clint closed her door and went down the stairs. He looked as he always did. He looked like a cleverly disguised pirate marauder.

When Wallis reached the top of the stairs, Clint was just at the bottom, obviously waiting for her descent. But before he saw Wallis, the front door opened to a covey of gorgeous women who were noisy and laughing. They shrieked to see Clint!

Wallis then watched him. He was very obviously appalled! And her humor was touched.

She saw as he took a step backward and his mouth opened in shock. He pulled himself up, eyes darting around, and he tried to shrink narrower to be alone and untouched.

Clint did that?

The women didn't even notice. They flooded over Clint, reaching to hug him, to kiss him. Chattering among themselves and talking to him. And they laughed as he caught their hands and turned his head away, missing most of the kisses.

That wave of women went on to take off their wraps and repair their makeup.

His horrified glance went up the stairs, but Wallis had drawn back just in time to avoid him seeing her.

He swore to God if no other woman spoke to him, ever, he'd be pure the rest of his life.

Men do desperate things in a crisis.

He took his pocket handkerchief out and rubbed his face free of lipstick and looked up to see Wallis about five stairs above him, watching him with pleasant interest.

She said, "You cut a pretty wide swath."

He knew a swath was cut by a tractor, so he recognized the pretty wide part. That part was like a white-hot branding iron on his bare butt.

She took his hand and with her other she rubbed lipstick off his chin as she said, "What you've done before this time doesn't count. But what you do after this . . . will."

That was clear enough.

Humor came into his eyes, and he asked, "Got your apron tucked up?"

She snootily nodded, but she had to control a grin.

Greatly relieved, he put her hand in the crook of his arm and said, "Don't leave me alone."

She laughed. He didn't say he wanted her around for his delight, only that he needed her for protection. She told him, "I just need to know if I'm the only one for you."

"Well, hell, you're the only one I want around...
permanent."

"I won't tolerate any temporaries in the meantime."
Then she added, "Or later."

"Got it."

It was an interesting evening. It took the entire span
of time for the unattached women to understand that
Clint wore a brand. How impossible! And they teased
him and chided Wallis. "How could you?"

"He saved me from a puma. You should have seen
him coming down that riverbank on Frankenstein! He
was magnificent! What else could I do?"

And one replied coldly, "Let him alone."

Wallis laughed.

She wasn't jealous. Renata and Margot exchanged a
communication considering that fact, then they nodded to each other. That's when Wallis became family to
the female part of the Covington household.

The whole evening, Clint was very careful in the most
courteous manner. He was kind, but he belonged to
Wallis. She knew it, but he was making it public.

So what more could be proven? They'd never quar-
reled. What would happen if ever they disagreed? What
if she made him so angry that he'd lose his temper and
infuriate her?

And as the days passed and Christmas approached,
it seemed that there would never be a really serious ex-
plosion between them. Until the day that she went out
in the Jeep she'd been assigned to search out more of
her grasses.

She had all the survival equipment, including one of
the satellite gadgets if she got into trouble. All the pre-
cautions were taken. She ignored taking someone along.

She'd told Clint, "I've always gone alone. If someone comes along, I get distracted and chat."

"Learn not to chat."

"How'm I gonna do that?" She was incredulous... and unbending.

So when Clint went to settle something or the other, she didn't wait for him to accompany her or find someone who would be willing to tag along. She just went.

She said, "First time, charm." And she removed the required hat and let the wind blow her hair. The top of the Jeep was up. The rugged vehicle would go anywhere, and she took off at a speed that tried the roads and her ability to bounce. She was... free!

Wallis hadn't realized, until then, how confined she'd been since Clint had rescued her from the river bottom. And she was shocked she'd been such a lily-livered wimp.

As she drove rather too rapidly, she sang out loud, and she was careless with the Jeep. They can turn over on a sharp curve. She had one scary recovery that warned her, and she was more careful, for a while.

But she reached the area where some of the oldest grasses had been discovered mixed in with the Johnson grass. She pulled the Jeep under some mesquite trees which, in time, the cattle had trimmed up like green umbrellas. The cattle liked the long, sweet, yellow mesquite beans.

Wallis got out of the Jeep and stretched her body. It was good to be by herself. She'd been crowded and cared for too closely. She liked being cared for, but she wanted the feeling of independence.

She took the holster from the Jeep and put it over her shoulder. It looked very like a canteen and didn't weigh much. She was used to it. And she remembered when she'd taken out the snub-nosed gun and said, "Bang!" to Clint.

He hadn't flinched or jerked or anything. It had been a stupid thing for her to've done. He had been grim about the silly act. Could she tolerate the stern supervision of a protector like Clint? She sat on the fender and looked around, thinking about Clint Terrell.

Once he got used to being in love with her and felt more secure, would he lighten up a little? How could she help him to hold her a little looser in his iron grip?

As she slid off the fender and began to look, she was distracted by her mental debate seeking a solution to his need to dominate, to be in charge.

She remembered the old saying: Begin as you plan to go on.

Perhaps the fault lay with her. She had been mesmerized by his easy command and ability. He was a man. He was all man. He expected to treat her as he would a woman he cherished. She didn't want to be so closely cherished. She wanted to help defend the fort.

Maybe her parents had raised her too self-determined.

No. It was her own doing. Her own personality. And she thought of all the women who yearned after Clint. The problem was that she understood them. She could be the same way with Clint. She had been. She just hadn't had any competition at the shack.

Ahh. What a man.

If he needed to protect her and monitor her for his own sake, she'd just have to adjust and allow him to believe she was that submissive. Could she? She'd have to see.

She went back to searching the grasses as one sought a specific color amid colors.

* * *

So they came on her with such ease. There were two of them. They had an old souped-up pickup, and in the back, they had parts of a freshly killed beef with a good deal of rolled fencing. The beef had been a sideline.

They were startled to see her. She looked at them and realized they were strangers. Being sideways to them, she foolishly thought she looked like one of the hands and turned her back to continue her search.

But they stopped the truck.

A plane was going over, and she wondered if it was one from the ranch. Could they see this far down and know the pickup was a stranger's?

The two men got out of the truck and stretched, looking around at the horizon and into the trees. There was no other person anywhere around. No cattle, no herders, no Leo, no Clint. Just her. The independent woman who wanted no supervision from any man.

One asked, "Watcha doing 'way out here all by yourself, honey?"

The other said, "Maybe we ought to go on along."

Wallis agreed with that and told the first man, "Listen to him. If you two are smart, you'll get back into that truck and sneak out of here, right now. This is Covington land, and there are some hard-nosed men who will take it very seriously if you don't leave immediately."

The first one smiled and lounged like a man does when he considers himself a lady-killer. "We just want a little drink from that cute, little canteen."

"Stay back. I mean it." And she lifted the black snub-nosed gun from the canteen-looking holder.

"OOOhhh, she's got a mean, nasty gun!"

She agreed. "And I can shoot it. Get back in your truck, right now, and leave."

The second man said, "Let's go."

But the first one laughed. "A little, bitty thing like that can't shoot a big, nasty gun like that."

So she shot right between them and deliberately hit their truck. They didn't notice that part.

"Now, listen here, honey, you hurt one of us and it'll go bad for you."

"It'll go worse for you. I'm giving you the chance to get out of this, unhurt. The next shot is right between your eyes."

From the shelter of the mesquites, a voice growled, "If she don't shoot you, I will." It sounded a little like Peanut, the huge, rough stable man.

Wallis didn't turn. She kept the gun on them. And Leo came up silently to stand between her and the two men.

"We didn't know she had company. We'll just go along."

"No." The voice was steely. "The sheriff is landing just behind you. You're in for a big surprise. Our hands trailed you. The beef ain't so bad, but they're madder'n hell about the fencing."

And the pilot revved his motor as the plane came up close. It had, indeed, landed on the road. Two men got out and whistled shrilly.

The rough-voiced one in the trees whistled back.

And other whistles around also responded. The two men had been hunted down, and it was happenstance that Wallis had been in the middle of it.

Clint was one who had emerged from the plane. He looked hard at Wallis and then went about the business of directing the other men.

The two culprits were cuffed and taken in. One of the ranch hands drove their truck and made a big show of being helpful to the two thieves in volunteering to drive the truck. He said, "It's against my grain to drive a tacky mess like that-a one? Glory be, my reputation'll be ruint."

Clint declined a ride back to the house and stood stonily waiting for the rest to depart. He had looked at Wallis and he had asked her, "Are you all right?" But he hadn't spoken to her again.

The other men had bragged on her, saying she'd really distracted the two thieves, and she'd sure scared them with that mean gun. But the posse could have probably gotten them without her help, although they did appreciate any assistance that came their way.

They did all leave, and only Wallis and Clint were left there in that very wide, open space. There were just the two of them . . . and Leo.

She petted the dog more than was necessary and then finally looked at Clint.

He returned her look. Then he slowly pushed his Stetson to the back of his head. He did that deliberately as she watched. He was angry—with her. He was warning her to be careful.

She asked with interest, "How did you know I would need you?"

Through thinned lips, he replied in a terse manner, "I saw you from the plane. I was afraid you'd be hurt or dead by the time we landed."

Her eyes were wide and her lips soft. "How strange. I was fantasizing someone in the plane would rescue me. That's like my dream of a man on a black horse rescuing me from the puma."

He retorted rapidly in unfiltered words. There wasn't his usual hesitation as he had censored his speech. This was his automatic response to stupidity. He was serious and intense as he verbally lambasted her, but he made no threatening moves. He was furious, but it was all verbal, and she understood this was how he reacted to stupidity. To carelessness. To something dangerously done.

She wasn't offended. She was mesmerized. Some of the words were in another tongue. His verbal fire could have seared the varnish off anything. Since she had no varnish, she survived.

She listened with attention. And that's what caught him. She wasn't afraid or angry or rebellious, she was alertly interested.

His words came to a halt. He stood there looking at his love. He said, "Wallis, my God, if anything happened to you, I'd die."

And she replied, "I understand. We've melded. I am sorry you were upset. As you know, I could have handled it all. You don't have to worry about me. But, Clint, you are magnificent. You awe me. You are so self-reliant that you should understand my need to be independent."

"You have to listen to me, Wallis. You have to obey the rules. There are rules out here, and the men all obey them. You have to know that rules are all that make this world work. When rules break down, so does civilization. You've seen it happen on TV in other countries and even here, in this one."

"Yes." But that was only an I-hear-you acknowledgment. Then she said the important thing. She said to that irate, frustrated, chancy man, "I'll love you all the rest of my life."

He stood with his hands on his hips as he studied her stonily.

She was relinquishing him. She thought she'd probably ruined everything between them, but she could not buckle down to the obedience he expected of her.

She watched him. Her eyes memorizing him. She was sadly, ruefully grateful she'd known him even so briefly. He was not a man to be crossed. But she was incapable of submitting to the authority of another.

He resettled his Stetson and looked at Wallis. Then he removed his hat and put it on the hood of the Jeep. Slowly he came to her.

She wasn't really sure what he intended doing. She waited with calm curiosity.

He took her into his arms as if she was fragile porcelain, and he held her to his hard body as he groaned. "My God, Wallis."

Then he kissed her.

* * * * *

Silhouette Desire brings Lass Small's devoted fans A NUISANCE, another sexy, fun-filled Man of the Month in January 1995. Be sure to meet confirmed bachelor Stefan Szyszko (pronounced Cisco) and roving reporter Carrie Pierce as they find their way to love in a town called Blink, TEXAS.

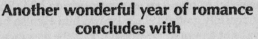

MILLION DOLLAR SWEEPSTAKES (III)

SILHOUETTE®

Desire®

M of the A N Month

More Great Reading From
LASS SMALL

If you enjoyed Lass Small's AN OBSOLETE MAN, December 1994 *Man of the Month,* you'll want to join her in January 1995 as she brings her devoted fans A NUISANCE—another delightful *Man of the Month.*... Only from Silhouette Desire!

Be sure to meet confirmed bachelor Stefan Szyszko (pronounced Cisco) and roving reporter Carrie Pierce as they find their way to true love in a town called Blink, TEXAS!

CHILDREN OF

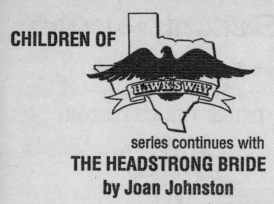

series continues with
THE HEADSTRONG BRIDE
by Joan Johnston

Rancher Sam Longstreet knew Garth Whitelaw was
responsible for his family's troubles. And he set out to even
the score. Sam planned to sweep young Callie Whitelaw off
her feet and marry her. But he hadn't bargained on *loving*
his headstrong bride!

Look for *The Headstrong Bride*, book two of the
CHILDREN OF HAWK'S WAY miniseries, coming your

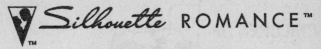

Silhouette ROMANCE™

'Tis the season for romantic bliss.
It all begins with just one kiss—

UNDER THE MISTLETOE

Celebrate the joy of the season and the thrill of romance with this special collection:

#1048 ANYTHING FOR DANNY by Carla Cassidy—Fabulous Fathers
#1049 TO WED AT CHRISTMAS by Helen R. Myers
#1050 MISS SCROOGE by Toni Collins
#1051 BELIEVING IN MIRACLES by Linda Varner—Mr. Right, Inc.
#1052 A COWBOY FOR CHRISTMAS by Stella Bagwell
#1053 SURPRISE PACKAGE by Lynn Bulock

Available in December, from Silhouette Romance.

SRXMAS

presents

WATCHING FOR WILLA
by Helen R. Myers

Willa's new neighbor was watching her.
Her every move, her every breath. With his
mysterious past, Zachary Denton was an
enigma. He claimed he only wanted to
warn her, protect her—possess her. And
like a butterfly drawn into a deadly web,
Willa could not resist his mesmerizing
sensual pull.

But was he a loving protector—or a
scheming predator?

Find out this February—only from
Silhouette Shadows.